ENDLESS DEVOTION & NEBULAS

AVA WIXX

WICKED Press WIXX

Endless Devotion & Nebulas

First Edition: October 2023
Published in the United States of America by
Wicked Wixx Press.
The Wicked Wixx Press Logo is a trademark of
Wicked Wixx Press.

Cover Art, Ava Wixx Logo, Wicked Wixx Logo, & Interior Book Graphics by Lindsay Tiry of LT Arts
Edited by Melissa Ringsted of There For You Editing

Print ISBN: 978-1-955950-12-1
Kindle ISBN: 978-1-955950-13-8
EPUB ISBN: 978-1-955950-14-5

For more information visit: avawixx.com

Yes, I was still doing this.

Though she thought herself weak, she is strong...

... GUIDED BY HER HEART'S UNWAVERING SONG.

Introduction

Once upon a time, humans thought they were alone in the Universe.

They were wrong.

Hundreds of thousands of species existed that weren't indigenous to Earth. So many, it was thought that no one would ever discover or catalogue every species and subspecies out there in the big, wide open.

Humans also used to think they were at the top of the food chain.

They were wrong about that, too.

Sexual, racial, religious discrimination … it all stopped mattering once humans realized they were the only ones who saw the difference. A human was a human, no matter their creed, and the rest of the Universe didn't have high opinions of the natives of Earth.

Long story short …

Humans had been long overdue for an awakening, and they'd been scrambling to survive ever since they got one.

In hopes to compete with alien races that were superior physically and mentally, humans began to splice their genes to create hybrids. New humans were born, and the rules changed yet again.

Battles waged and large casualties were amassed, including the loss of entire planets. So an alliance was formed, simply known as the Unified Galactic Federation of Stars or UGFS. It would govern all so chaos would no longer reign supreme.

Of course, that's when things really got complicated …

Official UGFS classifications:

- Species Class 4: Unknown species, unknown abilities.
- Species Class 3: Registered species, offensive abilities.
- Species Class 2: Registered species, defensive or benign abilities.
- Species Class 1: Registered species, no abilities defensive or offensive.

Galvraron: (Class 1) Genius species. Highest IQ among any discovered species. Blue-tinged skin. Humanoid.

Mazatimz: (Class 2) Species of healers. Lavender hair and eyes. Humanoid.

Metzas: Bonded pair of Mazatimzs. Combined skills vary.

Guaviva: (Class 2) Species who can speak to machines. Childlike in appearance. Black eyes. Silver-toned skin. Humanoid.

Talsen: (Class 3) Species of warrior-like males. Humanoid.

Denard: (Class 4) Not much known. Thought to be Humanoid.

Gartian: (Class 1) Creators of Gartian grade alloy, the strongest alloy known to any species. Humanoid, although appearance is unknown since the infection of G-Pox.

Spliced Humans or Hu-mutts: (Classes 1 -3) Humans created on New Earth. Human DNA mixed with alien species, resulting in varied classifications and abilities.

Chapter 1

Light glinted off the scalpel, my eyes riveted as it swooped down to hover over my abdomen. Sweat trickled down my temples, a grunt of protest escaping my bound mouth. I wanted to look away, but I couldn't.

Pain sliced through my stomach as the tiny blade did, trapping a scream in my chest. My body jerked upward on the table, bowing at an awkward angle in a bid to escape the agony forced upon it. I squeezed my eyes shut. I didn't want to know what was coming next, because there would be more. Even when I passed out, there was always more.

I jolted awake, gasping for air. *Another nightmare.* But it was different than the others. It wasn't me strapped to that table, but *him*. Even while trapped within the dreamscape I'd known the body I gazed down at wasn't mine—it was his. Someone so familiar to me I would recognize—

No. I shook my head, not wanting to think about *him*,

the loss too great to bear, time having dulled none of my anguish.

"Tamzeaaa!" Jane's slurred voice wafted through my locked door. Her steel-toed boots kicked against the barrier between us, repeatedly, with aggression.

Ah-ha. So that's what woke me. Groaning, I rolled over and stuffed my face into my pillow. "What now?"

Jane, my superior as captain and owner of The Pittsburgh, the ship I served as a healer on, had been hitting the firejuice hard while her phoenix mate, Ash, was out on a dangerous mission without her. Ash let her know beforehand that their mental connection would be rendered temporarily useless, which translated to late-night drunken visits from Jane of the paranoid kind.

At first, I thought it was cute, the 'rough around the edges' spliced human going all gooey because she'd been blindsided by her intense love for Ash, but that was before she refused to let me get a good night's sleep.

Having recently discovered her human DNA was combined with a phoenix's, Jane floundered when it came to knowing what to expect from herself emotionally and physically, especially now that she was bonded with a full-blooded phoenix. *Understandable. But exhausting for everyone involved, especially me.*

"Tamzea, please! There's something wrong with Ash's mate mark! I need you to check it! I think … I think Ash is in trouble! Please." A loud thump preceded a guttural sob.

My heart clenched. Even after almost a week of Jane's late-night visits, and me being borderline delirious, it was in my nature to soothe—to heal in any way possible. I could never ignore a plea, even a drunken, paranoid one, such as Jane's. The worry she felt was real, and therefore I had no choice but to help her. It was the curse of my kind, the curse of being born a Mazatimz. *Funny how I used to think of it as a gift.*

Staggering from bed, I lurched for the control panel, squinting my bleary eyes as I punched in the code to unlock my door. As soon as it slid open, Jane crawled forward on all fours, her bare back exposed in the dim lighting.

My eyes widened. "Why aren't you wearing a shirt?"

Jane collapsed on her stomach at my feet, her nails scraping along the metal floor as her fingers curled, sending a shiver up my spine. "I was trying to see Ash's mark. I was trying … and something's wrong." She twisted her head around to peer up at me, her eyes out of focus, and her long, golden-brown hair partially obscuring her face. "Just look at it, please."

"Yeah, yeah, fine. I'll check it out."

Dropping into a crouch, I gathered enough energy to probe Jane for any signs of trauma. If something was bad enough to manifest physically in her mate mark, I would be able to sense it.

After a moment, I rolled my eyes. Just as I expected, there was nothing amiss. The iridescent design covering her back from the nape of her neck to her tailbone was just as it always was, along with her internal energy fields.

"Well, what is it? You're awfully quiet back there. Just get it over with and tell me what's wrong."

"There's nothing wrong with you or your mark." *At least physically.* Pulling myself to my feet, I grimaced as a wave of vertigo hit me. "Now, will you please go sleep it off so I can get some rest, too?"

Jane curled into a ball on the floor, covering her head with her arms. "I can't lose him. I hate it. I hate loving someone like this. It's exactly why I never wanted … well, I never wanted anything beyond a good fuck with him. Or anyone. Look how pathetic I am now. But I can't … I can't lose him. I wouldn't be able to go on."

Anger coursed through me, heating my blood. I snatched Jane by the shoulder, wrenching her to the side so I could make eye contact. Her gaze wobbled back and forth in an attempt to focus. "You'd go on. You'd go on because that's what you did before Ash, and that's what you'd do after. Loving him so much it hurts, and worrying about him doesn't make you pathetic, but saying you wouldn't be able to go on definitely does." I let her go, sudden worry that I'd hurt her replacing my anger. I rubbed my temples. "Now, please, Jane, I need some sleep." It wasn't like me to be harsh, and it didn't sit well with me.

She lumbered to her feet, her eyes narrowed, flames dancing behind her irises. "What would you know? Huh? You've never—"

"Out!" I yelled. "Out now!"

Blinking rapidly, as if trying to process my sudden outburst, Jane finally took the hint and swayed in the direction of the door. "Fine. I'll go. I think I still have half a bottle of firejuice ..."

I shut and locked the door behind her, heaving a sigh of relief. I loved Jane like a sister, but her human half's dramatics could be trying at times. *I really don't know how pureblood humans survived as long as they did.*

Flopping back onto my bed, I was asleep almost as soon as my head hit the pillow.

"WHERE ARE WE GOING? *Where are they taking us?" I pressed my nose into Eron's neck just below his ear, inhaling. His spicy scent was my only comfort at the moment, that and the way his strong body surrounded mine.*

"I don't know." His breath tickled the side of my face, causing goose bumps to erupt.

"I'm scared."

"We'll be fine as long as we're together. As long as we have each other, we can survive anything, I promise."

I moved my face down to his chest, pressing my cheek into sculpted muscle. He was fitted in nothing but a silver pair of skintight shorts, allowing me to feel the warmth of his bare skin on mine. I was wearing not much more, silver shorts and a matching band of material that wrapped around my breasts.

Tipping my head back, I gazed at the pale chiseled face I knew almost as well as my own. Long, lavender hair framed a square jawline and high cheekbones. His lips were wide and full, almost feminine, and yet nothing else about him was. He wasn't traditionally handsome, considered too rugged among my people, who generally preferred gentler-looking males. But to me, he was nothing short of perfection.

Eron and I had been practically inseparable since birth, born hours apart. Rare among our kind, we were Metzas, two souls whose healing magic complemented each other perfectly. Together we could do things that most Mazatimzs could only dream of, and we'd fallen in love, which was rarer still.

"Why hasn't anyone come for us yet?"

Eron's grip tightened around me, his heartbeat thrumming erratically beneath my ear. "I don't think they know we've been taken. I don't think—"

"That's enough," a raspy female voice spat moments before I was yanked from Eron's grasp.

Panicked, I swung wildly, my elbow connecting with something solid, not bothering to see who or what it was as pain shot up my arm. I only had one thought: Get back to Eron.

"Tamzy!" Eron reached for me just as a large humanoid dressed all in black grabbed him around his waist from behind.

"Eron!" I thrashed, bit, kicked ... but no matter how hard I fought, I couldn't escape my captor.

Eron's eyes darkened with fear as he was dragged in the opposite direction as me. "No!" he bellowed. "You can't separate us! You don't understand!" He managed to get free for an instant, a singular moment in time, racing for me as I continued to struggle, my eyes locked with his.

He staggered, arching at an odd angle, before hitting the metal floor with a painful-sounding thud where he lay utterly still. The humanoid ambled forward, retrieving a thin cylinder from Eron's back, and then hefted him up and over his shoulder. Eron hung limply as if dead, although I knew he wasn't.

Gasping for air, I found none. My vision danced with black spots, which I attempted to blink away. A high-keening sound filled the air. Eron …

Jerking straight up in bed, I yanked my damp sheets away from my body. My living quarters wavered behind the twin shields of dancing water in my eyes. I blinked rapidly, trying to stave off the tears. *Twice in one night. What's going on? It's as if my brain is determined to force me to think of him.*

What I'd told Jane was true. If you lose someone you love, you go on, but you never *move* on, the difference only discernable to those who've experienced such loss. Every passing moment is a struggle to keep going, knowing that a part of you will remain empty for the rest of your life. I'd lost Eron. He'd been ripped from my life, but never my heart. What Jane and the rest of the crew on The Pittsburgh didn't know was that I was on the run, too —from my past, an inescapable thing.

I rubbed my open palm over my chest in an attempt to soothe the dull ache. I could heal so many things, even within my own body, but I could never fix what was wrong with me. A broken heart was irreparable even for a skilled Mazatimz such as myself.

The dim lights in my room flashed to red, The Pittsburgh lurching sharply, sending me tumbling from my bed. The ship's alarm blared, Zula's muffled voice coming over the intercom yelling something I couldn't quite decipher.

My stomach dropped into my feet as I struggled to pull my boots on. I didn't deal well with intense situations other than the medical kind, and ever since Jane had gotten herself mixed up with the Denards, we'd been careening from one frightening encounter to another.

Hurrying into the corridor, I made my way to the control room hoping to find out what was going on.

"Zula! What's with the alarm ... and everything?" I waved my hands around, motioning to the flashing red lights.

"Some kind of pod, escape I think, rammed into us, throwing us off balance." Zula gritted her teeth, furiously punching buttons on the ship's main computer consul. "Masha took care of the slight malfunction, which was nothing more than the impact setting us into a spin, and now I'm attempting to ensnare the culprit in our tractor beam."

Relief flooded me. Masha, our engineer, was a skilled Guaviva, and if she claimed to have our ship under control then I had no doubts. Despite that fact, I chuckled nervously. "Good thing The Pittsburgh is fitted with Gartian grade alloy now or—"

"Someone crashed into my ship?" Jane swaggered into the control room, her face flushed with anger. "You get 'em yet, Zula?"

"About to," Zula mumbled, her short blonde hair swinging forward to obscure her face.

Jane flopped down in the captain's chair, taking a robust swig from a bottle of firejuice. I leaned over and snatched it from her.

"Hey!" she protested, making an attempt to get it back, her reaction time impaired causing her to be entirely too slow.

"No, Jane. You've had enough. And don't you want to be able to stand up on your own when we nab whoever crashed into us?"

She slumped down in her seat, mumbling something I took as agreement.

Zula slapped her hand against the monitor in triumph. "Got it!"

"Great job, Smurfette!" Jane lumbered to her feet, swaying noticeably.

Zula shot Jane a death glare, speaking through gritted teeth. "I told you not to refer to me by archaic Earth words or terms. Just because I have blue-tinged skin and blonde hair—"

Jane cracked her knuckles and grinned. "Now let's go see who had the nerve to take me and mine on in a dinky little pod ship."

Delivering Zula a wan smile, I trailed after Jane, knowing Zula wouldn't be far behind us.

Chapter 2

"Those two are the ones who crashed into us?" Jane swiped a hand down her face, leaning against the secondary door to the airlock. "I must have drunk more firejuice than I thought. They look like kids …" She turned to face me, grimacing. "And they look like Mazatimzs."

Zula lifted onto her tiptoes, peering out the small window into the airlock herself. "Yes, the humanoid appearance combined with lavender hair and eyes does point to them being Mazatimz children. And they seem to be alone."

A fine tremor ran up my spine, temporarily freezing me in place. Mazatimz children, alone and in some kind of escape pod? Unless something happened to their parents or guardians, there was no way they'd be left on their own. There had to be some kind of mistake. *But you and Eron weren't the first, or probably the last, kidnapped for your abilities.* Mazatimzs relied on tight security, and if breached … well, my kind did not excel at fighting. It simply wasn't in our nature.

Forcing myself into action, I shouldered Zula out of the way, my stomach twisting with anxiety. Sure enough, huddled together on the floor were two Mazatimz children, both female, no older than ten, guessing from their slight frames and youthful faces. The clothes they were dressed in were non-descript, loose, and an off-white color, making it difficult to judge if they were malnourished or not. The small pod they had been in was barely bigger than they were, which was why it was easily brought in with our tractor beam. They must have hit The Pittsburgh at the perfect angle to set us into a spin. It was pure bad luck … or maybe good luck for them that they'd found me.

Slamming my palm against the keypad, I fumbled to get the door open. Jane snatched at my wrist. "What are you doing?" I hissed. "We need to help them." My gaze was riveted on the children. Their presence ripped open wounds and drudged up memories better left forgotten. I shook my head. *Get it together.*

"We haven't scanned them or the pod yet," Jane said, her gaze softening as she studied me.

"I don't care!" Flinging her hand from me, I fumbled at the keypad again, my fingers stiff, making it difficult to get the numbers right.

"Let her go," Zula murmured, stepping forward to punch the code in for me.

The door slid open, my ears popping as the pressure equalized, and the next thing I knew I was in front of the children on my knees, peering into their eyes. Lacking the finesse I usually had, I shoved my energy into theirs, testing and assessing. They held perfectly still until I was done, obviously aware of exactly what I was doing.

"You're okay. There's nothing wrong with you."

The smaller of the two girls smiled at me sweetly. "We could have told you that."

"Now, you need to tell me what you two were doing in that pod all by yourselves." An image of Eron flashed in my mind, and I shook my head to dislodge it. First the nightmares, and now unbidden memories of Eron ... *What the hell is going on?*

The other girl's lower lip began to tremble. "Our f-father put us in that pod and sent us away. He said it was the only way ..." Fat tears slid down her face, her grip tightening around her apparent sister.

I eyed the two girls with new appreciation. Twins, although not identical. I probed the bond between them, acknowledging what I'd already sensed on some level. They were Metzas. *Maybe that's why I've been thinking of Eron?* And being Metzas meant that they should have been guarded, protected with—

Like you and Eron were? My gut twisted. The way Eron and I had been stolen away from our people had been surprisingly easy. I, of all Mazatimzs, knew the flaws in our security.

Not wanting to push them at the moment, I stood and

offered my hands. "Come on, let's get you some food and then we can talk."

The smaller girl took the offering of my hand, squeezing my pinky and ring finger tightly. Her sister clung to her, swiping at her tears as if embarrassed by them.

Jane and Zula smiled encouragingly at the two girls when we passed from the airlock into the ship, although Jane's expression was forced. I didn't have to be a mind reader to know what she was thinking. Jane was wondering what we were going to do with them. A valid question, even I had to admit.

Even before the threat of the Denards constantly loomed over us, we weren't a child-friendly ship. Jane was a bounty hunter, and we often housed criminals because of it. In fact, we currently had a Class 4 locked up in the prison, being held for a day or two until we reached our rendezvous point where we'd be rid of him and receive payment. Although it'd never happened before, there was always a chance of escape since no things in life were certain, not even Zula's containment grids.

Lost in thought, I blinked in confusion when I realized we were already at the entrance to the eating lounge. I led the girls over to the large table and sat them down. Jane and Zula traipsed in a few moments later, the two of them lingering near the entrance warily. I fought the urge to laugh. Big, bad, bounty-hunter Jane, and I'm-smarter-than-everyone Zula were nervous around children. Somehow it fit perfectly.

Grinning, I said, "Come on in, Mazatimz children don't bite." Neither one of them moved. Rolling my eyes, I returned my attention to the girls. "First, I should probably introduce myself. I'm Tamzea." I nodded in Jane and Zula's general direction. "Ignore those two for now."

"Oh, for God's sake." Jane strode forward and gave a little wave. "I'm Jane, the captain of this ship. You know, the one you sent into a tailspin when you—"

"Jane." I shoved my elbow into her side, grimacing at having to do so. I disliked inflicting pain of any kind, but Jane had a way of forcing my hand, so to speak.

"We don't understand what she said," the smaller girl murmured, twisting a piece of hair around her finger.

Surprise widened my eyes. "How is that possible? Are your translators broken or malfunctioning?"

"We don't have translators."

I was rendered speechless. It was mandated by UGFS law to have translators implanted in all registered species soon after birth. Reflexively, I ran my fingers over the tiny bump behind my ear. It didn't make sense for anyone to not want such a thing for their children. It would limit their ability to understand—

Unless …

Another unbidden memory skittered across my brain.

I awoke suddenly, a blinding light shining into my eyes. When I attempted to sit up, I came to the horrifying realization that I was strapped down to a metal table.

"Grab her head," a female voice commanded. "The sooner we get this taken care of the better."

"I don't understand why it's necessary to remove their translators," a second female voice said, higher in pitch.

"Because that way we won't have to worry about them overhearing what we say. Plus, they won't get very far when the only language they'll be able to understand is their own."

"Yes, Mother."

My head was wrenched to the left, although I didn't put up much of a fight. I was worried that more than my implants would be damaged if I did under the circumstances.

Two slices of a blade, and the use of an extractor followed by a cauterizing tool, and I couldn't understand a word my captors uttered.

My thoughts returning to the present, I eyed the girls speculatively. "When were they taken from you?"

"Taken?" they asked in unison, tilting their heads in confusion.

"Yes, when were your translators taken from you?"

The smaller girl, who I was learning quickly was the more confident of the two, answered, "We never had any."

My feet and hands tingled, a wave of dizziness washing over me. "Where … where is your father? Why did he put you in that pod?" Before my knees could buckle, I flopped down into a chair across from the girls.

"He's in the only place we've ever known. With the bad people. The people who—" The girl clamped her mouth shut suddenly as if she remembered she wasn't supposed to say anything.

Zula sat down beside me, her gaze roaming over the

twins like they were a puzzle she wanted to solve. "Ask them their names again."

"Okay. Okay." I scrubbed a hand down my face, wanting all of it to be a nightmare. I wasn't sure if I could deal with having to face parts of my past drudged up by the presence of the girls. I wasn't strong like the rest of my crew. I plastered a smile on my face, hoping it didn't terrify them. "Let's start at the beginning. What are your names?"

"I'm Xia," the smaller twin said, "and she's Tia." She motioned at her sister.

"Their names are Xia and Tia," I announced to Jane and Zula while pointing at the corresponding twin—although I wasn't sure why I was translating to them, since it was the twins who were currently language impaired.

Jane snorted and slapped a hand against the countertop. "No matter the species, mothers of twins, or heaven forbid triplets or something, have serious issues naming their kids. I mean look at Dar, Zar, and—"

"Jane, focus," I snapped. "This is not the time to be thinking about names. Obviously, something happened to Xia and Tia and we need to figure out what so we can help them."

"Ask them about their mother," Zula interjected.

Right. They'd mentioned their father, but no mother. "What about your mother? Is she with your father?"

Xia shook her head. "We never met our mother. It's always been just our father."

Standing, I moved over to see what I could offer them for comfort food. We were low on rations, planning to restock after we collected the latest bounty Jane had bagged. While I rummaged for something young Mazatimzs might enjoy, I continued to talk, since I was the only one the twins could understand.

"What else can you tell us about where you were? Is your father in danger? We want to help you, so the more we know ..." I pulled out vanilla wafer cookies, my attention temporarily diverted. Technically they were from Jane's Earth food stash, but I'd been sneaking them, and I had a feeling the girls would enjoy them as well.

Smiling, I placed the tin of cookies on the table, shoving several in my mouth to put Xia and Tia at ease, even though they did seem to trust me already.

"Are those mine?" Jane hissed.

"We can get you more." I grabbed another cookie, nibbling on it as I asked, "Please tell me about your father. What's his name? And do you know where you were exactly?"

Xia snatched several cookies, offering one to Tia who took it hesitantly. "We don't know much. But the place where we were was called Telvin, and our father's name is Eron."

Nausea rolled through me, and my vision wavered. *Telvin. Eron. No. It's impossible. It has to be a coincidence. There's no way—*

A little girl's scream met my ears just as everything went dark.

Chapter 3

Weak. I have to pretend I'm still weak.

I had no idea how much time had passed since I'd been brought to this place, even though I wasn't sure where here was. Without my translator implants, I was only able to garner bits and pieces of information. It felt like years since I'd last seen Eron or any of my kind. I was kept in a small, sterile room that only housed a cot for me to sleep on, or rather collapse from exhaustion on, and a tiny private bathroom that held a shower, toilet, and sink. The only other room I'd seen was what I thought of as a laboratory. There my blood was drawn daily, and sometimes bone marrow. Those were the easy parts. The rest—I shuddered—the rest was too gruesome to let my mind dwell on.

I have to get out. I have to escape and find Eron.

Lately, my captors had been lax with me, secure with my docile and broken act. I may not be a fighter, but there were other ways—there were always other ways.

Waiting for the lock to turn on the outside of my prison, I scurried to the toilet and spit out the drugs they forced me to take nightly. No one questioned my consumption of the pills when I acted the same.

I simply had to wait for an opportunity. I hoped and prayed for one every second of every day.

"She's coming to." Jane's voice penetrated my consciousness as I was yanked from my painful memory.

"There was nothing wrong with her physically. Something emotionally traumatic caused her brain to shut down to escape," Tia's timid voice wavered as she explained my situation.

Groaning, I sat up, greeted by the sight of what I liked to think of as my office, the hospital, or medical wing. I met first Jane's and then Zula's concerned gaze. "I know you can understand them, but we need to make it so they can understand you … and everyone."

Jane grunted. "Just like a damn Mazatimz to be thinking of someone else right after— You dropped like a rock and scared the crap out of us!"

"I wasn't worried. Concerned a bit, but not worried," Zula stated. "You were the only one worried, Jane. Well, and the twins were worried, too. Although I suppose that's a Mazatimz trait."

My lips curled up despite the situation. "Nice to know you care, Jane." Our brash captain cared a lot more about her crew than she wanted us to know. It was a defense mechanism for her. She wasn't fooling any of us, though, least of all me.

I swung my legs over the side of the cot, wobbling slightly as I made my way to a storage locker. "Xia, Tia, we need translators in you both right away. I want you to be able to understand everyone. And then we're going to finish our talk."

Grabbing two sterile packages of translators from the locker, I turned to face the girls. Luckily, I kept spare translators on hand because Jane had a habit of damaging hers and I'd had to swap them out more than a few times. The procedure, when done by a Mazatimz, was painless and completed within minutes.

"Who wants to go first?"

Xia stepped in front of her twin. "I will."

"Okay, just sit on the table and turn your head."

AFTER INSTALLING the translators in the twins, exhaustion finally caught up to them. They were both sleeping fitfully on one cot tucked into the corner of my living quarters. I'd offered them their own room, but they'd insisted on staying close to me, which was understandable under the circumstances. I was a Mazatimz and familiar to them in that way alone.

I gazed down at the sleeping girls, studying their features. *Do their eyebrows have the same slope as Eron's, or is it just my imagination? And what about the strong, straight line of their noses, is that Eron's stamp on their genetics, or more wishful thinking?*

Because if Xia and Tia were *my* Eron's children then that meant he was alive. The fact that he'd possibly fathered offspring with another female was irrelevant. If he remained a captive of Telvin, then he might have been forced to create Xia and Tia, or they could have been part of an experiment. With what I knew, which wasn't much, anything was possible. *Even the Eron who is their father not being* my *Eron is a possibility. After all, the name is pretty common for Mazatimz males.*

I wanted so desperately for Eron to be alive. The day I'd escaped from Telvin was the day I'd discovered he was dead. *But I never actually saw the body.* I'd pulled up his file within Telvin's system, searching for a clue on his whereabouts, and— The image of 'deceased' scrolled across his file in big red letters nearly caused me to join him in grief. And yet, I'd managed to go on—to escape.

"No. What did I do?" My knees suddenly weak, I sagged onto my bed, my mind reeling.

Did I leave Eron behind to suffer all these years? What about our connection? Wouldn't I have felt him at some point? I turned my focus inward, searching for any signs of the invisible tether that was our Metza bond, but came up empty. I wanted to believe he lived, even if it meant I'd abandoned him, but a part of me felt it was impossible.

Pulling myself slowly to my feet, I crept over to the sleeping girls, swirling my hands through the air around them. If Eron was their father, then I should be able to recognize the feel of his energy within them. Until a

Mazatimz has fully matured, the energy of the parents' genetics lingered within every cell.

Strong Metza power zinged along my skin, jolting me. The twins would be formidable healers when they grew up, almost as talented as Eron and I had been on our way to being. But that was all I picked up on—a heaping dose of healing energy, no confirmation or denial of their genetics in regards to Eron.

Pushing a wave of calm and relaxation into the girls, I was confident the pair would sleep without nightmares or wake for at least a few hours. I had no idea what kind of horrors they'd suffered at the hands of the Telvin people, although I had a pretty good idea.

I have to talk to Zula. She'll help me figure this out.

My thoughts centered around Eron as I went in search of Zula in a fog, blindly clomping through the halls of The Pittsburgh, hoping to stumble upon my genius friend. Jane was good for brawn, and any kind of action. If I needed a reckless plan carried out, she was my girl. But Zula helped me see past my emotions to analyze situations, something that was difficult as a healer. I wasn't rash like Jane, but I felt so much all the time. *And at the moment I'm about to have a meltdown.*

"Where are you going?" Zula's voice broke into my haze, halting me abruptly.

Swiping a hand across my eyes to brush away the brimming tears, I gave her a tiny, relieved smile. "I wasn't going anywhere in particular. I was looking for you."

"It's about your past, isn't it? You've never talked about

it, and ever since those girls arrived …" Zula eyed me speculatively. "Where do you want to talk?"

Shifting, my eyes darted around, taking in my surroundings. We were near the medical wing. *Figures my feet would bring me here automatically.* "We can talk in the infirmary." I turned, shuffling along, knowing Zula would follow.

Before we'd reached our destination, Zula began pelting me with questions. "What do you know about those girls? Do you know what was done to them? Why would they be left vulnerable? I was taught that Mazatimzs, especially children, are kept under lock and key. If—"

"Stop. Okay? I'll answer all of your questions, but you're going to have to let me talk. And I will." I slumped onto a cot, Zula doing the same directly across from me, her eyes sparkling with curiosity. "I'm the one who was looking for you, remember?"

Zula shifted forward, perching her elbows on her knees. Although she remained mute, waiting, impatience rolled off of her in palpable waves. I expected no less. It was her eagerness to solve any puzzle presented to her that would aid me in my plight.

Exhaling a long breath through my nose, I nibbled on the inside of my cheek, pondering where to begin. "I've been running from my past. I didn't just yearn to get out into the Universe like so many of my kind get the itch to do. I was never meant to leave my home, I … we were too valuable. And yet," I choked back a sob, "we, my Metza and I, were stolen so easily."

Zula leaned back, surprise twisting her blue-tinged features. "Metzas. You are half of a Metza pairing. But where—"

"I thought he was dead. Killed by the same people who took us." I swallowed around the huge lump in my throat. "But now I'm not so sure. Now I think that Eron may still be alive and he may also be the twins' father."

She nodded. "And you couldn't sense it either way."

Zula was already putting some of the pieces together. It was nice that I didn't have to explain every little part like I sometimes had to do with Jane. Not that Jane was stupid, but she was distracted easily, and she would never be a Galvraron. "Yeah," I whispered. "I don't know what to think."

"And your emotions, the thought of the other half of you possibly being alive when you thought he was dead, has you—freaking out, as you would put it."

"Exactly."

Jane snorted from behind me. "I don't know what you needed to talk to her about, it's clear what needs to be done. We need to go find out if this Eron guy is alive."

I hung my head. "How long have you been back there?"

"The entire time," Jane retorted, laughing. "You were walking around like you'd been the one downing firejuice all night, and I had to find out what had you in such a tizzy."

"It's not that simple, Jane," Zula said, frowning. "We can't just go—"

"Sure we can." Jane moved forward into my field of vision, a huge grin stretching across her face. "And of course we are. We're not letting Tamzea sit here and angst over the possibility that the love of her life, who she thought was dead, might still be alive."

How does she know? "I never said he was the love of my life. All I said was that he was the other half of my—"

Jane rolled her eyes. "You didn't have to. It's obvious." She quirked one dark eyebrow. "You going to deny it?"

My gaze darted away from hers. "No."

"All right then. Let's start planning this rescue mission pronto."

Although grateful to Jane for taking the reins, I wasn't sure if it was more for me or for her, to keep her distracted while Ash was away. Not that it mattered. I knew, even if mostly motivated by selfishness, Jane would always have my back. The whys didn't matter, only the outcome.

My gut twisted, and my heart rate accelerated exponentially. Soon I'd have my answers about Eron, whether I truly wanted them or not. I wasn't sure if I was ready to find out that he was dead all over again.

Please let him be alive.

Chapter 4

"Well, do you think you can figure it out?" I hovered near the airlock door, not wanting to get in the way.

Masha was chest deep inside the engine of the pod the twins had arrived in, extracting the navigation system so the ship's course could be backtracked to its point of origin. Dar loomed over her, his shiny metal arm glinting as he twisted to hold the light where it was needed. He no longer wore what I'd come to think of as typical Gartian gear, which was a combination of their alloy and leather. He'd adopted similar tastes to what all of the crew on The Pittsburgh liked to wear: all black. Except for Jane, of course, who preferred the flamboyant look of Steampunk clothing. It seemed as if Dar had decided to stay aboard The Pittsburgh with Masha permanently. Things like the change in his clothes were little clues to his state of mind. I wasn't surprised. They were a perfect match, Guaviva and Gartian. One communicated with machines, and the other was more machine than Gartian male.

Moments passed and neither of them answered or so much as acknowledged my presence. "Hello? I asked you two a question."

"I thought it was rhetorical. Of course, my Masha can figure it out." Dar's lips twisted into a smile of indulgence and pride, causing jealousy to spike inside of me. Eron and I once shared a relationship much like theirs. We'd been a team, a perfect match in every way. *When did you let yourself start thinking about him so freely? Don't even think his name. Nothing has changed. Not really. Just because there's a chance—*

"Tamzea?" Xia murmured, her voice rough from sleep.

I glanced behind me to where the twins stood hand in hand. Their large lavender eyes studied me warily. *How are they awake? I thought I ensured a healing sleep.* "What are you two doing up? I told you rest was the best thing for you at the moment."

"What is he?" Tia asked, her gaze riveted on Dar. "I've never seen anything like him before." She broke away from Xia, moving forward as if in a trance. "His energy is …" She glanced back at Xia who nodded.

"I feel it, too," Xia whispered, moving towards Dar with the same gleam of awe in her eyes. "He's so different. It's almost as if—"

"He's a Gartian," I interjected. "Have you ever heard of them?" They both shook their heads slowly, neither of them looking away from Dar. "Their kind was infected by the Denards with something called the G-Pox, and it almost wiped out their entire species. The ones that survived became like him, a cyborg."

"Cyborg," Xia and Tia repeated the word as if learning it, and filing it away for later.

"He was created by the Denards like we were," Tia said.

A chill ran up my spine just as the light Dar had been holding clattered to the floor. "What did you just say?"

Tia tilted her head in confusion. "You said the Denards infected the Gartians with the G-Pox, which means they made him what he is, just like they made us what we are. Was I wrong?"

"And what are you?" Dar asked, his gaze intent.

"Important to them," Tia said.

"Which is why our father sent us away," Xia hastily tacked on.

Dar moved forward in a blur, crowding me. "We can't take them anywhere near this Telvin place if what they say is true."

My nostrils flared as I pushed aside the panic growing within me. *No. I have to know if Eron is alive or dead.* "Are you suggesting we leave their father in Telvin to rot? Not to mention we have no idea what or who else they have there. I was a captive there once myself, and I can't begin to describe the horrors of such a place."

Dar inched closer to me, his hot breath fanning over my face. "If they're important to the Denards we need to find out why. We can't risk handing them over."

"Dar, please." Masha tugged on his arm, averting his attention. "You're scaring Tamzea and the twins."

"What has the Gartian's panties in a twist?" Nina strode into the room, blonde head held high.

Even though Nina had saved Jane from certain death by way of Ambassador Aralias, Nina's now-dead ex-husband, it didn't change the fact that she was a Denard herself. Sure, she'd been tortured by her own husband, the pattern of scars crisscrossing her face a constant reminder, but some forms of prejudice and hatred were difficult to overcome. Despite Nina's want for revenge on her own people because of how she was treated, Dar didn't want Nina on the ship, and because of it, Nina enjoyed antagonizing him. The best Jane had been able to do was make them swear to not hurt each other physically, therefore insults were regularly hurled back and forth between the two of them.

"No one asked a Denard scum like you to speak," Dar hissed, turning towards Nina.

Nina opened her mouth to lob a retort when one of the girls screamed, the sound forced somehow. Whirling around, I saw Xia and Tia dart hand in hand behind the pod, trembling with fear. I had about one guess what had them quaking in their tiny boots.

"Nina, you need to leave. They're afraid of Denards. They just came from a facility run by your people, and it—"

"Say no more," Nina snapped, even though her expression had softened. "I'll leave, but for them, not because of the Gartian." She pivoted on her heels and promptly left.

Wasting no time, I made my way to the twins. They were huddled together behind the pod, eyes wild with terror. Before I could do or say anything, Dar appeared beside me.

"I won't let any Denard hurt you." He reached out both of his hands in an open invitation to Xia and Tia. Surprisingly, they didn't hesitate to accept, and once their tiny hands were encircled by Dar's massive ones, he leaned down and said, "But you're going to have to tell us everything you know about the place you were held. Everything. We don't have time to wait for you to feel more secure or comfortable. This is very important. Do you understand?"

They nodded in unison.

I wanted to chastise Dar for putting so much pressure on them, but I knew he was right. With the knowledge of the Denards being involved with Telvin came the urgency to move more quickly. We needed to find out exactly why the girls were so important to the Denards.

I knew what I had to do. "I'll get the information we need. Bring them down to the medical wing now, Dar."

PRESSING my palms into my closed eyes, I inhaled and exhaled deeply in an attempt to settle myself. It'd been years since I'd done anything like I was about to do with the twins. Even if I messed up the process, there would be no long-term side effects for the girls, but my mind could end up mush, my consciousness lost within theirs. There was no name for the Mazatimz mind blending process, for it wasn't a common practice. Only Metzas such as Eron and myself were even told of the process anymore.

Shit. I don't think I can do this. Not without Eron. I dropped my arms and opened my eyes, focusing on the doorway as Dar's boots echoed off the metal floors. At any moment he'd enter with the twins, and I'd have to decide whether or not I was going to proceed.

Dar stalked through the doorway, balancing one twin on each of his hips, Masha trailing along behind him. "Where do you want them?" Dar asked, his eyes burning with some unknown emotion.

I have to do this for Eron. For my people. For all of those who have been abused by the Denards. I'm worth the risk. One life for the many. "Just set them down on one of the cots."

After depositing the twins on the cot closet to me, Dar and Masha turned to leave. "Wait!" I exclaimed. "Stay. I need you to stay. Someone has to be here in case something …" I glanced at Xia, her lavender eyes locking with mine briefly. "I just need you both to stay." I couldn't bring myself to say out loud that something might go wrong, and if I ended up an incoherent vegetable, someone was going to have to comfort the twins in the wake of my failure.

Dar nodded in understanding, pulling Masha into his side as her black eyes widened with alarm.

"Thank you," I whispered.

I sent up a silent prayer to Aceso, a Goddess of Healing that I read about in one of Jane's Earth books. My people worshipped no higher power, believing in only the tangible ability of medicine and healing, but at the moment, I'd take any little bit of help I could get.

Plastering what I hoped was a pleasant smile on my face, I knelt in front of Xia and Tia. "I'm going to go into your minds to look for things you might not understand that could help us. It won't hurt, I promise."

I smoothed Tia's hair back with my left hand, resting my palm on the crown of her head, before doing the same to Xia with my right hand. Normally I would only attempt merging with one person's mind at a time, but as Metzas there was an invisible tether between the two of them and it would be easier to use that to my advantage. Luckily, I understood the bond since I was one-half of a Metza pair myself. At least I used to be.

Closing my eyes, I inhaled deeply, gathering my energy. "Now think of Telvin. Think of it and your father." *Am I really doing this just for a chance to know if my Eron is alive sooner than I would have otherwise? Maybe.* But the rest was true, too. With the involvement of the Denards, we had to know everything possible, and sometimes children see and hear things they don't think important. That's what I'd be searching for.

I delved into their minds with my energy, linking the three of us together. A kaleidoscope of colors exploded behind my closed eyes, settling into a scene.

Before me on a metal table, lay a burnt and deformed humanoid, at least from what I could tell. I was only able to observe what the girls had seen, and at the moment the dying creature was the only thing taking up their vision.

As if I was there with them, the acrid scent of burnt flesh crept up my nostrils, causing bile to rise into my throat. *I'm too far in, I need to take—*

"Xia, Tia," a heartbreakingly familiar voice stole my attention. "You must heal her."

I felt both the girls' emotions simultaneously. Hate, disgust, fear ... They didn't want to help the monster lying on the table. She was a Denard, cruel and heartless. She'd hurt them and their father more times than they could count.

"Look at me."

Yes, look at him. Show me once and for all if I merely want Eron to be alive so desperately that I'm hearing things or if it's real. Show me!

Xia and Tia turned reluctantly, their gazes averted. Xia said, "We don't want to help her."

"And we don't even know if we can," Tia added.

Strong fingers tipped the twins' chins upward, filling their vision with their father's face.

My body trembled with joy and relief, guilt and sorrow. Eron, *my* Eron, stood in front of Xia and Tia, very much alive. I was so overwhelmed, I didn't notice the changes in him at first, but slowly they crept into my consciousness as I observed him in the twins' memories.

Eron's eyes, although not altered in color, seemed

darker, cold, and hard. They no longer held hope of any kind, merely resignation. His long, wavy hair had been shorn off, leaving only about half an inch of his lavender tresses all over his head. His features were sharper, harder. He'd aged just like I had, but … but something was missing within him. My heart twisted, dropping into my stomach.

"You must heal her." Eron's jaw muscles popped as he ground his teeth together. He didn't want the girls to heal whoever was on the table any more than they wanted to. But still he pressed. "If you become useless to them you know what will happen."

Fear washed over Xia and Tia, replacing all other emotions. "Yes, Father," they murmured in unison. "We'll heal her."

Eron's head jerked up, his gaze trailing along the ceiling of the small room as if he could see through it to track something moving above. "No. It can't be. It—" His eyes slid shut, a fine tremor moving down his body as he clenched and unclenched his fists. "Tamzy, you're alive." When his eyes snapped open, they flashed with a torrent of varying emotions before they went flat once more.

He grabbed Xia's hand and swung Tia up onto his hip. "Change of plans. It's time for you two to get out of here."

"Father?" Tia's voice wavered with uncertainty, her tiny hands clutching at his shoulder.

"You have to listen carefully to what I'm about to tell you. Not all of it will make sense, but you can't disobey me, not even for a second. Do you understand?"

The twins nodded as Eron dashed down one hallway that blurred into the next because of his speed. "Good, good," he whispered to himself before continuing. "I'm going to put the two of you in an escape pod, and I'm going to need for you to follow someone's energy thread, someone like us, a Mazatimz."

"But how?" Xia asked. "How are—"

"I'll show you when we get to the pod how to direct it. It'll be simpler that way. The most important part is that you lock onto this energy before it gets too far away. It's going to feel like mine, but slightly different. This person is connected to me like you're connected to each other. Do you understand?"

"Yes," Xia replied, her eyes wide and transfixed on Eron. She'd never heard of her father being linked to another in the way she and Tia were. Would it be his brother or sister? Did he have a twin, too?

"But when you find her, you have to hide who you are. You have to hide your genetic energy as I showed you before."

"Why, Father?" Xia asked.

"Because she can't know I'm your father."

"But why?" Xia demanded.

"Because if she knows, she'll come here to save me, and she can't come here. Ever."

Xia and Tia glanced at each other and nodded, silently communicating. They would do what their father demanded, and find the other half of his Metza pair, but they wouldn't obey the rest. They couldn't just abandon him. He was their father and they loved him. Once they knew for sure that they had found their father's Metza, they would reveal exactly what he didn't want them to so that he could be rescued, too.

And they knew just the way.

Yanking my hands away from Xia and Tia, I collapsed on the floor, dark spots dancing in front of my eyes. "You manipulated me. Made me think this was my idea. You've been playing with all of us from the beginning." A sharp laugh escaped my throat. "You could have just told me, you—"

An image of Eron's face wavered in front of me. It was the last thing I saw before I fell into oblivion.

Chapter 5

"Eron, please don't go," I murmured, twisting my fingers into his hair, tugging him towards me.

I sighed in bliss when his weight settled over me, and his lips skimmed along my jawline. "I have to go."

"No. Stay."

"Your parents, as much as they love me, will not appreciate finding me in your bedroom like this."

I wrapped my legs around his back. "We haven't done anything ... yet."

"I ca—"

"They're going to be late tonight. The council had some issues arise, issues that could take all night to solve. I heard my parents talking about it before they left."

Eron's strong fingers danced up my arms, interlacing with my hands to pin them over my head. "Mmm ... I guess I could stay for a little longer then."

"Yes, stay." My breathing sped up when he pivoted his hips

against mine, warmth spreading through my middle. It was more than just the physical sensation of the way he touched me, it was his power merging with mine. It was as if in those moments, we were one, and yet remained two separate entities.

His lips fiercely devoured mine, his tongue sweeping in to take control of my mouth. Yes. I love you, Eron. And I want to feel more. Please give it all to me.

Sensing what I craved through our emotional tie, Eron broke away from me, his gaze meeting mine with surprise and lingering desire. "Tamzy, my Tamzy, I want it to be—"

"Don't you dare say special or something as cliché as that. Because you know it will be ... it's us, after all. Please, Eron. I don't want to wait until after some stupid bonding ceremony. None of that means anything, not to us. There'll never be anyone else for either of us, never has and never will be."

He quirked an eyebrow, a lecherous grin spreading across his face, showcasing both of his dimples. "Well, when you put it that way. Who am I to say no?" He tugged his shirt off over his head, throwing it to the floor.

Nibbling my bottom lip, I traced the indentations of muscle from his chest down his torso. I loved studying his masculine body and wanted to learn every inch of him. We were so close emotionally, and yet he was still foreign to me in so many ways.

"You're so beautiful," I murmured.

"No, I'm not like other males of our kind. I should never be described as beautiful. If it wasn't for—"

"Shut up," I growled. "If I say you're beautiful, then you are, at least to me." I punctuated my sentence with a sharp bite to his nipple.

Hissing, he delved his fingers into my hair. I flopped back on the bed a moment later, my gaze colliding with his. "No more stalling, Eron. It's admirable that you're trying to wait, but I don't want to. And I know you don't want to either. Not really."

He couldn't hide his true emotions from me. He was merely attempting to be noble for me. Something I didn't need or want. The only thing I craved was to be closer to Eron. There was only one thing left for us to do.

With an animalistic growl, he tore the remaining scraps of clothing from both of our bodies. "Tamzy, I ..."

Grabbing his erection, I tugged gently, guiding him to my entrance. He didn't need any further encouragement. Pressing forward, he entered me for the first time. There was a pinch of pain, but his healing gift soothed it away a moment later, leaving me to feel nothing but pleasure.

Our bodies and souls tangled in an intimate dance, one that I'd never quite been able to fathom. The reality of us joining in this way was so much greater than anything I'd imagined.

I trembled around him, my heart seeming to stutter just as all my nerve endings erupted in euphoria. Vivid colors exploded behind my closed eyes, Eron's name falling from my tongue with reverence.

"Tamzy, Tamzy, Tamzy," Eron muttered, the muscles in his neck straining. When he finally pulsed within me, another wave of euphoria slammed into me, this time darkening my vision.

Sometime later, as if the fog from my brain simply blew away, I found myself tucked against Eron's side, his strong arms holding me possessively. "Wow. I never ..." Clearing my throat, I attempted to string together a more coherent sentence. "That was ... wow."

Eron's laugh rumbled in his chest. "My sentiments exactly." He tipped my chin up with his index finger, his gaze snagging mine, intense emotion swirling within the lavender depths. "I love you."

I pushed up on my forearm, leaning in to kiss him gently on the lips. "I love you, too."

"I probably should go soon." He sighed dramatically, fisting my hair. "But now I never want to leave."

I giggled. "That was my plan all along."

Eron rolled me under him, his eyes darkening with fresh lust. "Wanna go again? I have a feeling things will get better with practice. Lots of practice."

"I do believe I've created a monster."

"Tamzea, you need to wake up," a familiar voice echoed in my mind.

I shook my head, not wanting to obey. *No. I can't. I don't want to leave him.* In that moment, I realized I'd been lost in a memory of Eron. It was one of the best ones I had of him. It was the first time we'd been intimate, and the last because a mere four days later was when he'd been ripped from my life.

I forced my consciousness back into the memory.

Inhaling deeply, this time I was aware that what I was experiencing wasn't real, which made me want to relish it all that much more. It was as if I was still there, the scent of Eron surrounding me as his touch lingered in all the right places.

"I love you, Tamzy."

"Wake up!"

"No!"

"You have to save him."

"No. I can't."

"If you don't wake up then all he'll ever be is a memory."

Tears slid down my face, anchoring me in reality. It was true. I couldn't live in the past, not when the real Eron was still alive. Not exactly waiting for me to save him, though. In fact, apparently, that was the last thing he wanted, but there was no way I could leave him behind a second time.

My eyes fluttered open for a brief moment, but I quickly squeezed them shut again to shield myself against the blinding light.

"She's going to be fine now," Xia said.

"Don't ever risk one of my crew like that again," Jane growled.

"We knew we could heal her or we never would have let her go into our minds," Tia murmured, her voice timid.

"Jane, calm down. She'll be fine," Zula chimed in.

Groaning, I opened my eyes again, sitting up slowly. I was flustered, my emotions ripped raw. I wanted time to process what I'd discovered in the twins' minds, but I knew I wasn't going to be given that option. "Jane, I'm fine. I just—"

She took me in her arms in an uncharacteristic display of affection. Her skin was hot, a sign that her phoenix was close to the surface. "You were completely unresponsive."

"I'm fine. I just had to—" I turned my head, glaring at Xia and Tia. "Well, I guess I didn't have to do anything. I would have been lost, my brain fragmented if they wouldn't have been able to heal me."

Zula squeezed my shoulder once before stepping away. "Luckily, they're very powerful."

A wave of dizziness spun my vision, my heart speeding up. "I'm sure Dar and Masha caught you up on everything? About the Denards being involved in Telvin?"

"Yes, they did. This information changes everything. Now that we know the Denards are involved, I have to say I agree with Dar, we can't—"

"Oh, we can." Jane flopped down beside me on the cot, flames dancing behind her irises. "I want at that place even more than before now that I know the Denards are involved."

Zula crossed her arms over her chest, scowling. "It's too much of a risk, Jane."

Their argument faded into the background, a slight buzz within my ears. Whether my crew decided to help me or not, I was going to rescue Eron. I would find a way to free him, even if it meant I ended up dead in the end.

Chapter 6

"Do it now. We both know you will eventually. Stop stalling. You have no other choice."

My hand trembled violently, the hilt of the long blade pressing into my palm painfully. My gaze swept over the young female Mazatimz strapped to the table. Fear filled her eyes, and yet she still trusted me on some level. She's a fool.

"It could just as easily be another Mazatimz. One you care about—"

A cry of frustration and agony ripped from my chest, and I plunged the dagger into the Mazatimz's heart. Surprise froze her features, blood bubbling from her mouth.

"That's right. I knew you'd do it in the end. You have no choice."

Dropping to my knees, I clutched at my head, screaming. I wasn't meant to harm. Only heal. Only heal. Only heal ... *The words swirled in my mind, taunting me. No matter the reason, who I sought to protect, I'd become a monster. I craved death, needed it, and yet ...* I have to keep her safe, no matter the price. I'll do anything for her.

"Tamzy." Eron's voice ricocheted around my brain, forcing me awake. Confusion held me tightly within its grasp for a few moments, the nightmare I'd been lost in horrifically real. I didn't know what it could mean.

My mind crystallized, and I jerked upright, my gaze darting around my living quarters. I was alone, the twins not asleep on their cot like they had been a few hours ago.

"Tamzy. I love you."

Squeezing my eyes shut, I willed the imprint of Eron's voice away, even as I longed to hear it over and over again. If we managed to rescue him, the Eron I knew, the innocent boy I'd grown up with and fallen for, would be different, forever altered. Telvin had held him captive for years, and there was no telling the emotional damage done to him in all that time.

It's my fault. I should have searched for proof of his death. I just left him there.

Would he blame me for abandoning him? As Metzas, I should have been able to sense him through our bond, and yet I hadn't felt anything. Nothing at all. How was I cut off from him completely? There were so many questions, and yet—yet ... *He's alive! He's alive!* No matter how many other sorrows came with that revelation, nothing could truly take away from that fact. Eron was alive, and soon, very soon, I would get to hold him in my arms again.

Standing, I lurched for the intercom. "Hey, anyone know where Xia and Tia are?"

"They're with me," Zula responded a moment later.

"Okay. Good. And how about the bounty? We have a new rendezvous set up yet?"

Jane's voice crackled over the line, "Bounty? What bounty?"

I rolled my eyes, even though no one could see it. "Seriously? The Class 4? The one we were on our way to collect payment on when the twins found us."

"Yeah, of course. The Class 4 in our prison. I thought you were talking about something else."

The line remained silent, forcing an exasperated sigh from me. Jane had clearly forgotten the bounty, which wasn't the first time, and she didn't want to admit it to Zula, who was surely stewing over it. Now getting information from them would be like pulling teeth.

"I'll just have to find out from Masha," I grumbled, flopping back down on my bed to pull my boots on. The sooner we dropped off the bounty and collected on him, the sooner we'd be on our way to Telvin.

My thoughts swirling around Eron again, I quickened my pace, dropping into a dead sprint when I reached the hallway. The combination of nerves and adrenaline wouldn't let me go any slower.

"Tamzea." Nina appeared as if from nowhere directly in front of me, and I let out a high-pitched shriek before skidding to a stop.

Clutching my chest, I leaned against the wall. "Don't do that!"

Nina grabbed my arm, tugging me away from the engine room. "I need to talk to you … in private."

"About what?"

"I—"

"What are you doing here? Didn't I warn you about coming into this part of the ship?" Dar loomed over Nina, causing her nails to dig into my arm.

Yanking free, I scowled at Dar. "Nina can go into any part of the ship she wants. You can't order her around."

"I don't want Denard scum like her—"

"Just stop!" I poked my index finger into Dar's massive chest. "Jane wants her on this ship. End of discussion."

Dar's lips pressed into a thin line, and his face flushed. Despite his posturing with Nina, he respected Jane. "One day Jane will wise up about her, and I'll be waiting." He pushed past us and continued down the corridor, his strides full of hostility.

I turned to Nina. "What is it you want to talk to me about?"

She grabbed my arm again, tugging me after her. "Not here."

"Okaaay." I glanced over my shoulder just as Masha exited the engine room looking for Dar. "How much time until we're at the rendezvous point?"

Masha reached out to touch the wall, closing her eyes for an instant. "Any moment," she said before hurrying off after Dar.

No matter how many times I saw Masha communicate with The Pittsburgh, it still managed to amaze me. She merely had to be touching any part of the ship, and the amount of information she could pull from it was astounding.

"We don't have much time," Nina mumbled.

"Time for what?"

"Here." Coming to Nina's quarters, she punched in her door code and hurried us through as soon as it slid open.

Once inside, she turned to lock the door. Her room was sparse, with no personal effects of any kind to be found. Snagging my attention was the intercom; it was disconnected from the wall, the wires hanging out to show exposed metal and plastic.

I pointed at the mess. "You don't have to attempt repairs yourself if you don't know what you're doing. Masha can fix that."

"No. I didn't want anyone to be able to listen."

"Tamzea!" Xia and Tia called in unison, their tiny boots pinging off the metal floors as they ran past the door.

I turned to leave, concern for the twins replacing my curiosity about what Nina had to say, but she grabbed my forearm, preventing me from leaving. "No. I have to—"

"I need to see what they want, we can talk after."

"No—"

Shrugging out of Nina's grip, I burst into the hallway. "Xia! Tia!" I called, the girls no longer in sight. I ran headlong after them, my heart thrumming loudly against my eardrums. Ever since the twins had crashed into The Pittsburgh, my already frazzled nerves had been eating away at my sleep-deprived mind. I was in a constant state of anxiety and uncertainty. *Maybe Jane's mood is wearing off on me.*

"Tamzea!" Xia stepped around the corner, her tiny hand linked with Tia's. Her eyes were wide, panicked.

My vision wavered, Xia and Tia's forms shimmering for an instant. I shook my head and clutched at the wall. "What is it? What's wrong?"

"You have to come with us."

"Why?" Bile rose in my throat, an image of Eron dancing in front of my mind's eye. *Get it together.* I turned my focus inward, searching for the reason why my system was suddenly out of whack.

"Please. You have to come with us."

"Yes, of course. Just give me a minute." My energy levels were off, lower than they should have been, dangerously low in fact. I concentrated on balancing them, while at the same time attempting to find the source of my energy leak. Shock rocked my system, and I whipped my head up to meet Xia's gaze. "You're stealing my energy. Why?"

The twins glanced at each other, a silent conversation passing between them.

I collapsed to my knees. "Stop. You're taking too much. You'll kill me." Normally I would have had no problem preventing any creature, even a Metza pair, from taking what wasn't freely given. But Xia and Tia had already breached my defenses. It was too late to fight them off.

"We won't kill you," Xia said. "We need you."

My eyelids fluttered, my body going numb. I wasn't sure if I was even upright anymore. "No. Stop," I muttered, my words nearly indiscernible.

Again I attempted to grab onto my leaking energy and patch up the hole in my shield, but everything slipped past me like water through my fingers, my efforts futile. My heart slowed, as if relaxed, my breathing deep and raspy.

"Don't worry, Mother, you'll be with Father soon."

What? Mother? What does that—

Everything went dark.

Chapter 7

My neck muscles strained, and my teeth gnashed as spittle flew from my lips. "No! I can't ... won't do it anymore."

Several sets of hands gripped me, forcing me onto the table as I was strapped down. My gaze swung around the room, wild and unable to focus. "I'm not meant to hurt. Only heal!" I roared.

A low laugh rumbled through the air. "You'll change your mind. You always do."

Steel rods pressed into my temples, fire burning through my veins. Biting my tongue as I resisted the urge to scream, blood filled my mouth, the copper tang all too familiar. In the recesses of my mind, where coherent thought somehow still existed, I wondered why I bothered to fight anymore. They broke me time after time. I told myself she was safe now, and that I could stop being their pawn. But they'd changed me, bent my will to theirs.

I didn't know who I was anymore, except a monster. And monsters only knew how to be one thing ...

My head throbbed, the scent of sterilization enzymes filling my nostrils. When I swallowed, the bland taste, gritty and disgusting, rolled down the back of my throat, gagging me. Confusion washed over me. I remembered what the twins had done, but I wasn't any closer to figuring out why. And what they'd said just before sucking the last bit of energy from me, forcing my body to shut down ...

None of it made sense.

On reflex, I immediately did an internal diagnostic. My energy levels, although still low, weren't life-threatening. Nothing else seemed amiss. Heaving a sigh of relief, I forced my heavy eyelids open, blinking foreign surroundings into focus.

Or maybe not so foreign, after all.

My breath caught in my parched throat as the small room came into focus. It was either the same room or eerily similar to the one I'd been kept in the last time I'd been a captive of Telvin. It held nothing more than a cot, and a tiny bathroom with a shower, toilet, and sink.

My past overlapped with my present as I remembered the first time I'd awoken in such a place. It had been at least a decade earlier, and I'd been sanitized, and stripped —both literally and figuratively—of my dignity. I shivered, thankful that my second go-round had at least left me with more clothes on, although not my black cotton pants and shirt combo I favored while on The

Pittsburgh. Instead, I had been dressed in light grey pants and a matching shirt. I might have lost my mind if I found myself in the same skimpy two-piece silver outfit from my first abduction experience.

A borderline hysterical laugh ripped from my chest. After everything I'd been through, I was right back where I started. And the twins had obviously brought me here. How, I wasn't exactly sure. Although they could have easily knocked out the rest of the crew and dragged me onto one of the escape pods since clearly, they had an agenda from the start. *Please let everyone be okay.* I would never forgive myself if my crew had become collateral damage because I'd blindly trusted Xia and Tia, forcing them to as well.

"Hello?" I called out. "Things are different this time. I have people who will find and fight for me. People who will save me." Jane, Zula, Masha, and even Dar wouldn't leave me here. *If they're alive. No. I won't let myself go there. They're fine. They're all fine. Focus on the positive. You're getting out of here. And soon.* My crew already knew the name of the facility, and with Zula's brain … "Just let me go and save yourselves the trouble."

A moment later, the heavy metal door swung open, and a large humanoid male was illuminated in the bright lighting from the hallway. My gaze snagged on his familiar face in horror. It was the same creature that had tormented me my first time in Telvin. I had no defenses against his brute strength, and something about his genetic makeup made it impossible for me to penetrate his body's energies. I didn't even know *what* he was, except large, deathly pale, hairless, and extremely imposing. His blood-red eyes only added to the intimidation factor.

Curling into myself, I shuffled back a few steps. "You can't do this to me. I'm a registered UGFS citizen, and I'm part of a crew. They'll come looking for me."

A slow smile spread across the humanoid's face, exposing large blunt teeth that were yellow. "Let them come. We could use a hu-mutt with phoenix DNA to play with. Not to mention the rest of your unique crew."

My mouth opened, but the words lodged in my throat. Of course I already knew where they'd gotten that information from. "Xia and Tia," I growled, finding my voice.

He stalked forward, maneuvering to grab me around the neck and waist from behind. "Such sweet girls. Must make you proud."

As he dragged me from the room, I flailed my arms and legs, knowing I wasn't physically strong enough to fight him on my best day, let alone when my energy was low, but not wanting to be complacent.

Bile and stomach acid intermingled in my esophagus, burning, our destination becoming apparent. Soon, I found myself in one of the two rooms I'd visited daily during my last stay at Telvin. The laboratory, as I dubbed it, held nothing but memories of pain, and the ghostly fingers of my agony trailed along my skin, causing goose bumps to erupt. I screamed, not from fear exactly, but from frustration. *How am I here again? After everything?*

With almost no effort on his part at all, despite me biting and kicking, I was suddenly strapped down to a metal table. Hot, angry tears slid down my cheeks.

"Now, now, don't cry." My tormentor swiped at my cheek in a mockery of tenderness. "This is going to be just like old times."

"Not quite," I snapped. "I can understand you." Not having translator implants when I'd been at Telvin before, I'd never even learned the creature's name. Not that I'd cared. I merely thought of him as just that … 'the creature.'

He chuckled. "That is exactly what I've been instructed to remedy first."

Shoving my head to the side, pain ripped through my skull, emanating from just behind my right ear. I ground my teeth together to keep from screaming. Warmth replaced the pain a moment later, my body healing the small wound before a cauterizing tool could be used. I was stronger than on my last visit to Telvin. Relief washed over me just in time for the same procedure to be done to the left side of my head.

Panting heavily, sweat trickled down my brow as I met the creature's muddy gaze, his eyes glinting with joy at my suffering. He said something to me, the words now lost in translation.

Grimacing, I spat, "Yeah, well I'm glad I can't understand you anymore. You didn't have anything important to say."

He slapped my cheek gently, laughing. He said a few more words before turning to leave. An instant later a shadow slid over me, and I craned my neck back to see—

"Eron!" My heart stuttered before setting off at a gallop, threatening to break free from my ribcage.

He stood motionless above me, his cold eyes dancing over my features as if I was a stranger. "You shouldn't be here." His voice sounded strange, monotone, and flat.

Fresh tears filled my eyes, distorting Eron's face, and I blinked them back furiously, raking my gaze over him with hunger. I'd seen the changes in him from the twins' minds, but witnessing them in person made the alterations in him real for the first time. A lump formed in my throat, and I struggled to breathe. "I thought you were dead."

He leaned over, his long fingers digging into my shoulders as he shook me. "You shouldn't be here. They promised me they'd leave you alone." Anger made its way into his voice, low and smoldering.

"I know. I know you sent the twins to me so they could escape, and told them not to tell me about you, but—"

"No. I never sent them to you. They did, and I should have known better. I should have known I couldn't trust them to keep their promise." He stepped away from me, a scowl turning down his wide mouth.

I reached out, searching for our bond, and found nothing. "Eron, why can't I feel you?" Ice raced up my spine. "What have they done to you?"

His head lifted, his nostrils flaring. A stranger gazed at

me from Eron's face. "I became what they wanted me to be. I became an abomination … to protect you. And now you're here!" he roared, the veins in his neck bulging. "You're here and there's nothing else I can do."

"I don't understand."

Eron slid his hand under my neck, grabbing my unbraided and tangled hair tightly, forcing me to look straight ahead. He exposed his left forearm, holding it inches from my face. There, branded into his flesh, was a tattoo depicting a snake of some kind. The mouth was open, fangs dripping venom. "This is to remind me of what I am now. It reminds me that I couldn't … can't fight them. Instead of healing, I poison. I'm like a snake in the grass. Creatures come here, and think they can trust me because of my lavender hair and eyes—they know our kind from reputation—but then I strike."

He let go of my hair, my head falling the short distance back onto the table with a dull thud. "This is what I am now. To survive, to protect what was most important to me, I had to lose what made me a Mazatimz. I had to become something else. A monster."

"Eron, please. Whatever you think you've become, they've made you that way. It—it … why can't I feel you?" I didn't want to think about the rest of what he was implying. Only then did I realize he had entered the laboratory unescorted, and on his own.

"You can't feel me because I turned it off. All of it." His voice had gone monotone again as he busied himself placing items I couldn't see onto a tray.

"No, when I was in Xia's and Tia's mind you felt me. I—"

"None of that was true. I already told you that. Those girls aren't what they seem."

"So they aren't genetically ours?" I hadn't allowed myself to truly think about the twins calling me Mother, or what the creature had alluded to either.

Eron expelled one long breath. "Yes, they share our genetics, grown in a test tube from pieces of us that were stolen. But trust me when I say, once you get to know them, the real them, you won't ever claim them as yours in any way."

"They're just children. And they're ours …" All the air left my lungs when Eron rolled the tray towards me, several large needles catching the light. My gaze flicked up to Eron's face. "What are you doing?"

"Being what I am now."

He picked up the smallest needle, sliding it into the crook of my arm without hesitation. The vial slowly filled with blood. I turned my head, not wanting to watch—it wasn't that I was squeamish, after all, I'd healed my fair share of gory injuries. It was knowing what was coming next, and that Eron, *my* Eron, was going to be the one to do it.

Screaming, I arched off the table as much as I was able when Eron plunged the largest needle into my abdomen. My stomach muscles spasmed, accompanied by a burning sensation as drugs were released deep within me. Spots danced in front of my eyes, and I willed my body to shut down temporarily. It was all too much to handle. He hadn't even bothered to use his abilities to take away the pain.

Eron, at least my Eron, might be dead after all.

I CAME TO SLOWLY, not wanting to face reality. Eron, my Metza, had not only hurt me physically, but he'd gouged out my heart with the coldness directed at me. It was something he shouldn't have been able to do. In the past, he would have rather suffered immeasurable pain himself than harm me in any way.

Maybe he really is something else now. The image of the snake on his arm flashed across my mind.

"I don't know what Father sees in you."

I jerked upright, my gaze flitting over Xia and then Tia. They sat cross-legged on the floor a few feet from my cot. I opened and then shut my mouth. There was nothing I wanted to say to them. They'd tricked and betrayed me. How they'd produced fake memories was beyond my comprehension, although I was sure that's exactly what they'd done.

"You're weak," Xia mused.

"And you're gullible, too," Tia tacked on.

Anger and indignation sizzled through my veins, heating my blood, and loosening my tongue. "It's called compassion. Something, as Mazatimzs, you should be acquainted with intimately. I saw two children who were lost and afraid, and I wanted to help them."

Xia tilted her head, studying me. "That's what makes you weak."

Swinging my legs over the cot, I leaned forward, digging my fingers into my thighs. "You two don't know the first thing about weakness, or strength for that matter. What would the two of you do if you were ripped away from each other, each thinking the other dead?"

The twins glanced at each other, before returning their gazes to me. "Father never thought you were dead," Tia said.

Xia nodded. "He's strong. You are not."

My mind circled back around to what the twins had said when I'd first awakened. "And you're wrong about your father. He sees nothing in me … anymore." Merely saying the words out loud caused my chest to tighten, the urge to curl into a ball overwhelming.

Xia snorted. "You're all that matters to him."

Reflexively my hands pressed again my abdomen, the pain inflicted by Eron gone, and yet the memory of it lingered. "You're wrong. He wouldn't have done," I swallowed around the lump in my throat, a flash of his emotionless eyes causing me to cringe, "what he did to me if that was true."

The twins stood, Xia taking Tia's hand, her small voice sharp. "Then you're even stupider than we thought." They whirled around, the door opening for them to step through, and then slamming closed.

I eyed the door, noting that I hadn't seen anyone open it on the other side. Did Xia and Tia have some kind of control device, or were we being monitored? Not that having the answer would help me in my current predicament.

Slumping back onto the cot, I stared at the ceiling, my gaze going fuzzy. My mind wandered, bits and pieces of information floating around in my head. I'd thought I'd been so smart, so clever when I'd escaped from Telvin. And yet, in hindsight, I realized it might have been entirely too easy, as if I'd been let go.

"They said they'd leave you alone." Eron's words ricocheted against my skull, alluding to a different story. Between my ease of escape, and how I'd stumbled across the report of his death, I knew there were pieces of information I was missing. *If I'd been allowed to escape, why was I brought back into the fold now? Had they somehow known where I was all along?* I shuddered at the thought. I'd been terrified to return to my home for two reasons: I couldn't face our families with the news of his demise, and I no longer felt safe there. My people had failed to protect us.

The twins are right. I really am stupid.

I'd wanted so desperately to believe I was safe with Jane and the rest of my crew on The Pittsburgh that I'd denied the truth, even if I knew deep down things hadn't been quite right. I'd abandoned Eron and left him at Telvin to endure unspeakable things. I was weak, a coward. I should have sensed he was alive. I should have saved him before he was lost to me forever, despite the fact that his heart still beat.

His scent, his taste, the way his skin felt under my fingertips, the way his pulse raced when I touched him … they were all things I could and would never forget. *If he's become something else, maybe he's better off dead.* At least before nothing tainted my beautiful memories of us together. Now, after one interaction, the new Eron's shadow darkened our past, negating a chance at a future.

Rolling over on the cot, I pressed my face into the rough material, inhaling the scent of sterilization enzymes. *No. You can't let this place get to you. Jane and Zula will come for you.* And if I got Eron away from Telvin, maybe I could save him, too.

Hope alighted in my belly, spreading warmth throughout my limbs. Yes, Eron might have changed, been forced by endless torment to be something else, but I could change him back. I would change him back.

Or I'll die trying.

Chapter 8

The minutes dragged by agonizingly slow, and me with nothing to do but think. I wondered how long until I'd see Eron again, something I both dreaded and looked forward to. The old Eron was inside somewhere, but the shell of his former self was terrifying. When someone you trusted turns on you, it makes it hard to believe in anything, even yourself.

And what about the twins? Eron confirmed that they were genetically ours, but they hadn't been conceived in love, and I felt no connection to them beyond the commonality of our species. It was hard to imagine ever feeling otherwise when they were the reason I found myself back at Telvin. *But then I never would have known Eron was still alive. And I would go through hell itself to save Eron, which is probably what I'm going to have to do.*

The door to my prison creaked open, the creature appearing with a tray in his hands. The smell of food swam through the air, delicious despite me not knowing what it was. I hadn't eaten since I'd been captured, hadn't so much as thought about food, but my stomach cramped, suddenly ravenous.

The creature dropped the tray at his feet, food sloshing over his boots. After a few words and a sneer, he slammed the door shut behind him. I lurched off the cot, falling to my knees to shovel the unknown cuisine into my mouth, barely tasting it. I topped off my meal with a tin of liquid, not water, but it quenched my thirst, which was all that mattered.

My vision blurred, and my tongue felt entirely too large for my mouth. *Damn, I've been drugged. I should have known. One stupid mistake after another.* Slumping to the ground, my eyes slid shut against my will. I couldn't help but think of Jane at that moment. I couldn't count how many times I'd wondered how she ended up in various ridiculous situations, taken captive several times herself. I'd thought myself smart enough to not make the same kinds of mistakes as the half-human. Suddenly, I was growing a new sense of appreciation for her survival skills. No matter what happened, she somehow always ended up on top. *Because she's cynical and suspicious, and generally a brat about having things her way ... Now I understand why.*

My heartbeat slowed, forced into false relaxation, my consciousness slipping, even my furtive thoughts lost in the drug-induced fog.

Nausea surged within me, my stomach pushing bile up my

throat. Outwardly I was calm, but inside my chest constricted in pain.

"Can Mazatimzs grow back limbs? Should we find out?"

I glanced furtively at my hand, each finger bent back, some with bones protruding. I sneered. "Kind of hard for me to do the surgeries you want if I can't use my dominant hand, don't you think?" A part of me wanted it to end, for death to swoop me away from my constant torment, but the survivor in me forced my acquiescence on a primal level. I fought, resisted still, and yet with each torture session, mine and others alike, I hardened a bit more, felt a little less. Soon I'd do what they wanted willingly, motivated by not wanting to suffer any longer. After all, whether I did it or not, the experiments would happen. And I knew deep down, death wouldn't come easy at Telvin's hands. Not for me at least.

"Then your other hand. Maybe just your smallest finger to start with."

My arm was yanked to the side, and my pinky finger placed within a cool metal vise. I arched a brow. "I don't know why you bother. I don't care what you do to me anymore."

"Ah, but what about her? You still care about her, don't you?"

Rage boiled my blood, dropping a red haze in front of my vision. I struggled to remain immobile, deceptively calm. Because I did still care about her. I would always care about her, even if my own life had lost its meaning.

"I'll do it," I growled. "I'll do whatever you want. You won't have to coerce me anymore. Just promise me you'll leave her alone. Leave her alone and you have yourself a willing pawn—a slave. I swear it."

Squeezing my eyes shut, I pictured her face, and a smile I'd never see again. She was all I had left. I had to preserve her life even if it meant sacrificing my very soul to do so.

A male and female voice wound their way into my waning consciousness, their words indecipherable, yanking me from yet another nightmare. Fear skittered over me, and I fought to move, much to no avail. My body was lifted, a feeling of weightlessness causing nausea to roll through my gut.

The male voice snapped something in annoyance.

"I said I'll take her," Eron responded, his tone flat.

I couldn't help but react to his voice. A sense of security, although misplaced, washed over me, pushing me further into the darkness threatening to claim me. I willed myself to fight my body's automatic response to Eron, but it overruled my brain.

"We'll be fine as long as we're together. As long as we have each other, we can survive anything, I promise."

Eron's long ago uttered words, some of the last few he'd said before he'd been ripped away from me, literally, played through my mind. They'd been true once, and I'd never doubted them until now. *No. That's not entirely true. My heart still trusts him even if my mind doesn't.* Maybe I had to give him my trust completely so he could live up to it. Like so many monsters that are created by the cruelty of others, possibly, all he needed was for me to believe in him to throw off the self-imposed shackles. For someone like Jane, who was partially human, the notion would be absurd, but I wasn't human, and neither were my emotions. I could do things that no partial human would ever be capable of.

I'll heal us both. As long as we have each other, we can survive anything. I'll make sure of it.

"TAMZEA, WAKE UP." A finger trailed down my cheek, pausing a moment before continuing its journey down my neck. "Tamzy ..."

Groaning, I opened my eyes to meet Eron's limpid pools of lavender. They were cold and hard, and yet something stirred deep down, a familiar softness. I thought I'd imagined the moment of tenderness before I awoke, but now I wasn't sure. "Eron." I licked my lips, surprised that I wasn't dehydrated. "What's going on?"

Reluctantly I turned my head to take in my surroundings, pushing past a wave of dizziness. I was strapped to a metal table, but surprisingly not in the laboratory. The aesthetics of the room were similar, but the ceiling was made up of glass, some sort of observation deck above us, where several empty chairs were situated.

"Now that the subject is awake, I will begin shortly," Eron said.

I watched as several humanoids, both male and female, filed in to sit in the chairs behind the glass, their gazes sliding over me with interest.

My breathing came out in short little bursts, and my

heart thrashed against my ribcage. "Eron, tell me what's about to happen."

His attention elsewhere, he muttered, "It's better if you don't know."

"Eron, pl—" I clamped my mouth shut, swallowing the words. I wouldn't beg. I'd told myself I would heal us, and in order to do that, I first had to trust in him, no matter the situation, and no matter how dire things seemed. "I trust you."

Eron's back went ramrod straight, and he turned slowly towards me, his eyes narrowed with anger. "Don't say that."

It wasn't the reaction I'd been going for exactly, but at least it wasn't cold indifference. I decided to press forward. "But I do trust you. Always have and always will. No matter what."

He gripped the side of the table, his gaze darting furiously over my face. "You wouldn't be saying that if you knew what I was about to do to you."

I licked my lips, forcing a small smile to curl them up. "We'll be fine as long as we're together. As long as we have each other, we can survive anything, I promise."

Eron blinked rapidly as if processing my words. His nostrils flared as he leaned into me. "Maybe that was true once, but not anymore."

It was in that moment, all of my recent nightmares clicked into place. It was painfully obvious, and I wasn't sure how I'd missed it before. I hadn't been able to sense the bond outwardly between Eron and myself, but when I slept, his memories had been seeping into my subconscious, showing me the mental and physical torture he'd had to endure at Telvin. It helped me understand the new Eron better and strengthened my determination to heal him at any cost. *But why only lately? What's changed recently when all of these years I got nothing?* Or maybe that wasn't true either. Some of my old nightmares hadn't made sense, but I'd thought they were my twisted memories, things my brain couldn't make sense of.

Pursing my lips, I forced myself to focus on the present, pushing my questions aside for the moment. "Do what you have to do. I know it's not your choice. Do it—just do it, and know I won't blame you because I trust you wouldn't hurt me if you could help it."

"Do you think you'll make things easier for me that way?" He bared his teeth, his expression feral. "I want you to hate me—hate me for what I'm about to do. If you do anything less," his voice cracked, "it might break me. More than I already am."

I bit my lower lip, wishing I could touch him. "I'm sorry, but there's nothing you could ever do to make me hate you."

A myriad of emotions played across his face before his features finally settled into an unreadable mask. Clearing his throat, he said, "I'm beginning the procedure now."

Picking up a wicked-looking blade, the scalpel's evil cousin, Eron placed the tool against my stomach. I forced my gaze up to his profile, pushing my fears aside. *It doesn't matter how much he hurts you, it's not his choice. You can get through this.*

Pain sliced through my middle, ripping a scream from my chest. I bucked against my bindings, unable to help myself. Sweat gathered on my face, and trickled down my brow. Yet, I was shaking as if cold. *I'm going into shock.*

Gathering my energy, I pushed it through my body in an attempt to heal as best I could. Mazatimzs could mend themselves to a certain degree, but they couldn't take away their own pain.

"What's the point of this? Any of it?" I managed through gritted teeth, tasting blood.

I was met with silence, no answers forthcoming, fresh pain blooming faster than I could heal the wound causing it.

More pain than my body could handle.

My eyes fluttered shut, my consciousness slipping away to a place of temporary peace.

Chapter 9

Soft, full lips skimmed my forehead, lingering a moment before pulling away. "I'm sorry. But at least you'll hate me now."

My eyelids too heavy to open, I muttered, "I could never hate you. You didn't have a choice."

"There's always a choice," Eron snapped, his hot breath fanning my face.

Inhaling sharply, I reveled in the spicy scent I'd long since been denied … *Eron. Home.* I yearned to comfort him, to heal. It was in my nature to help all of those in need, therefore the urge to soothe Eron, the male I loved, was a hundredfold what I normally felt. *Because I do still love him. No matter what, I always will.*

"No, you could have done some things differently, but there were no real choices for you to make. If you didn't do what they wanted, you'd probably be dead." Reaching out blindly, I found Eron, and I slid my fingers down his arm. Heat burned through my veins, the feel of his skin intoxicating.

"Make no mistake, I'll die here. And probably sooner rather than later."

"No—"

"Listen to me," he whispered in my ear, goose bumps erupting across my flesh. "I will get you out of here somehow. That's all I can promise anymore. Nothing else. Forget who I was before, the things I swore to you. Because there's no hope for me. I made peace with that fact a long time ago."

"No, I don't accept that. I won't leave Telvin without you again. Before I thought you were dead. I—"

"You're here for a reason. The twins are growing and maturing, and they want to understand their capabilities. But they're too important to test. That's why you were brought back. They want to test both of us. They think I haven't figured it out yet, but I know they feel my usefulness has reached its expiration date without you. Once I get you out of here, they will kill me."

"Then we'll both get out of here."

"You wouldn't say that if you truly understood what I've become—the things I've done. You should hate me. You will hate me by the time you leave."

Eron's heavy footsteps moved away from me, and still, I couldn't peel my eyelids open. A door opened and shut. Without Eron near me, I slipped slowly back into unconsciousness, no reason to fight the pull of oblivion any longer.

MY HEART WAS *a block of ice in my chest, cold and unfeeling, frozen around the only thing that kept me alive, although it was hidden deep.* Tamzy. *Thoughts of her both steadied my course and tormented me. If she saw what I'd become she wouldn't feel the same about me as she once did.*

An ear-shattering scream pierced my thoughts for a brief moment, my eardrums shattering and healing within seconds. My current victim was a hybrid, holding the DNA of a being once referred to as a banshee in human folklore. But the creature on my table was very real, and I was about to kill her.

I couldn't drudge up any emotions, except disgust for myself. I'd become nothing more than a walking contradiction, pieces from two incongruent puzzles forced together, but mismatched all the same. I yearned for one last time to hold Tamzy within my arms, and yet I hated the thought of her ever seeing me again. Hated that she'd know the monster I'd become. Thoughts of Tamzy kept me going and twisted my insides into knots. She was my savior and tormentor all rolled into one. I would always love her, but I'd grown to hate her a bit, too.

"Hold still," I grated, "this will only hurt for a second." The banshee's scream abruptly halted, her eyes dulling as death swept her away. The urge to heal her before it was too late bloomed in my chest, but it quickly faded, my gaze snagging on the snake etched into my forearm. It was pointless. All of it.

A clattering sound jolted me awake, and I tumbled off of the cot, adrenaline causing my heart rate to quadruple in time. Shaking off the lingering fog of my latest nightmare, which I now knew were Eron's memories, I realized there was a tray of unknown food just inside the door of my prison. As soon as the delicious aromas reached my nose, my stomach twisted with hunger. But after being drugged with my last meal, I resisted the urge to eat anything. I could go weeks without food if I had to.

I have to get out of here. I need a plan.

Although I hoped Jane would show up at any moment to rescue me, guns blazing, and yes it was quite plausible it actually would happen that way, I couldn't just wait around like some kind of damsel in distress. I'd read several of Jane's Earth fiction books over the years, and although I wasn't built for fighting, I had found the role of the inept female to be extremely distasteful.

One didn't have to be a fighter to be a survivor. I could be strong without being like Jane. Or even Zula. Everyone has individual strengths inside of them, even if it isn't the obvious kind. Some of us simply have to dig deeper to find our reserves. Or rather, maybe I was the damsel in distress in my current situation, as much as I hated to admit it, but that didn't mean I couldn't be my own white knight as well.

I first had to consider the facts. I had no weapons at my disposal, nor did I know why Telvin had renewed interest in me years after my escape beyond my tie to Eron. Of course, maybe it was that simple. Perhaps what Eron had guessed about wanting to test us was true. They'd created Xia and Tia from my and Eron's DNA, which wasn't surprising. I'd had blood, bone, and pretty much everything imaginable taken from me, although at the time I hadn't known what they'd planned to do with it. Now I found myself in the same predicament. I still didn't have the foggiest idea what Eron had done, or taken from me in my last torture session. By the time I could focus my energies enough to scan, I'd already been healed, which my body had done while sleeping.

I lifted my shirt, probing my stomach with my fingertips. Not even a scar remained. *Eron had to have helped. I'm good, but I'm not that good. Which means ...*

I searched for the tether, the tiny link that bonded me to Eron as my Metza. It was absent before, locked behind a wall of Eron's own making, the only time I could sense anything from him was when I was sleeping. But now ... It was faint. Barely discernable. So thin it threatened to snap at any moment, but it was there.

Sudden euphoria lightened my mood, making me feel buoyant about our future. All I'd done was tell Eron that I loved him and that I trusted him, and I'd already broken through to him. It may only be a crack in his shield, but it was all I needed.

I nodded to myself, dissecting the difference in his behavior from when I'd first seen him again in comparison to when he'd told me he would get me out of Telvin. He'd softened a bit ... not much, but enough to give me hope.

I gnawed the inside of my cheek, my eyes lingering on the tray of food my body so desperately wanted. I had no doubt more drugs were contained in the meal, so what would happen when I didn't partake? Surely I'd find myself forced into unconsciousness once more and without the joys of a few extra calories.

I can't keep going round and round like this. If I do, it will surely be my downfall.

Not eating wasn't the place to take my stand. My currently unformulated plan couldn't rely on deprivation such as that. I had to be strong, physically and mentally. An opportunity would present itself, I just had to be patient.

Decision made, I scurried on all fours across the room, using my hands to shovel the unknown cuisine into my mouth. I washed it all down with a dark red colored juice that had both sweet and tart flavors intermingled.

Leaning back, I waited for the drugs to take effect. Sure enough, a few moments later my vision blurred and my eyelids drooped.

So predictable. Why do they even bother with the pretenses?

Chapter 10

I came to where I'd expected: strapped to a metal table. This time I found myself back in the laboratory. It was a small reprieve to not have an audience for my torture. Much to my dismay, Eron was also absent. Instead, the creature loomed over me, a demented smirk curling his lips up, and beside him stood the twins, their expressions bored.

The creature said something to the twins, and they nodded, moving a few steps back.

"What did he say?" I demanded, directing my question to the twins. I hated not being able to understand him.

Xia scrunched up her nose. "If he wanted you to know then he would have told us to tell you."

"How do you still understand him? They let you keep the translator implants?"

"They only took them out to make our imprisonment

seem more believable to you," Tia said. "I thought that would be obvious."

Narrowing my eyes, I studied the twins with annoyance. Their faces held little resemblance to mine and favored Eron's traits, but translated in a feminine way. They both would be stunning when they matured, I had no doubt, and yet I wondered how my and Eron's genetics combined to make such brats. As Mazatimzs, and beyond that, Metzas, it should have been inborn to be kind, to want to heal. Only those with defects in their gifts turned cruel. As far as I could tell, both Xia and Tia had immense power, therefore they should have been … different. I had sympathy for them since they were children, and a kinship to some degree since they were the same species as me, but I felt no motherly instincts towards them, a fact that bothered me, despite their personalities. I'd never felt inexplicably drawn to them, and shouldn't I have?

The creature tightened my bindings, drawing my attention back to him and away from the twins. "Where's Eron … I mean, your father?" My gaze followed the creature's movements warily.

"Our father was asked to work on another new arrival," Xia snapped. "But don't worry, he won't be able to stay away from you for long."

Xia's tone confused me, although I'd heard it once before. Was there some kind of misplaced jealousy directed at me? Maybe Eron had never bonded with the girls, and as their father, they felt he should love them more than me. Perhaps some of their hate was because they felt abandoned emotionally by Eron. Or was it because I'd never been a part of their lives? Again, it was in Mazatimz's nature to be forgiving, but who knew what kind of twisted things had been brought out in the twins by being raised in Telvin? I yearned to pepper them with questions, but all curiosity about my children fled from my mind when pain—sharp and sudden, like fire burning through my veins—rocked my system.

I convulsed violently, tasting blood as I bit my tongue. Scrambling to heal, I gathered my energy, searching for the cause of my agony. *No, no, no, that can't be right.* There was no specific reason for my suffering. I was under some kind of mental attack, the likes of which I'd never encountered before, and I had a feeling who was responsible.

"Stop!" I screamed. "Please! Mazatimzs aren't meant to do this!" My only response was an intensifying of the burning. It scorched my insides, liquefying my organs. If not permitted to heal, I would die soon. My own children were killing me, and the thought brought me profound sadness as I slipped into a sort of delirium.

A loud crash echoed through my head, angry voices following. The burning was instantly replaced by ice racing through my system to soothe and repair.

I was denied the bliss of unconsciousness, hanging in a grey area of confusion, and yet not fully aware of what was happening around me. Someone lifted me, hefting me into their arms. Comfort and warmth surrounded me, and I pressed my face into smooth skin, inhaling. *Eron.* I would recognize his scent anywhere. I clung to him, not physically, since I was incapable at the moment, but emotionally. *I knew I could trust you.*

His lips brushed the top of my head, and words I couldn't quite understand whispered in my ear. None of it mattered, though, because I was with Eron—that's all that would ever matter.

HAVING FALLEN into a fitful slumber at some point, I groaned and stretched, feeling strangely refreshed. *Eron.* Jerking up, I found myself in a small room, but not the one I'd been kept in before. This one was slightly bigger, and instead of a cot, I was splayed across a large bed.

The bathroom door swung open, and Eron swaggered out, wearing nothing but a towel around his waist. Without meeting my eyes, he made his way over to the far wall where a closet was revealed when he pressed his hand against a panel there. Dropping the towel, he reached for fresh clothes.

Despite my current situation, and what I'd just been through, my breath caught in my throat at the sight of Eron's naked backside. He'd grown and matured since the last time I'd seen him without clothes, which was nearly a decade ago. Wide, muscular shoulders tapered down to a narrow waist, and his ass … well, my mouth watered with the desire to bite it. *I've been hanging around Jane too much.* Along his once flawless skin was a smattering of faded scars, the sight sobering my lustful thoughts quickly. *What did they do to you?*

Unable to help it, I stood, drawn across the floor like Eron's body had me caught in a tractor beam. I stopped just behind him, watching as his shoulders tensed, but he didn't turn.

"What happened?" I ran my fingertips from one scar to the next, gently tracing them.

"Too many things." Eron's voice was low and gruff, filled with pain … and desire, for me. He spun, capturing my hands within his. "I couldn't let them torture you like that anymore. But I was stupid. They weren't going to kill you. It was just another test within a test."

I swallowed, my gaze locking with his. "A test for what?"

"To see how strong our connection was—is."

"But why?"

"I have my theories, but nothing is confirmed yet." He swayed above me, leaning closer.

"Why am I here with you now?"

"Because they want you to be."

"Who are *they* exactly? I still know nothing more about this place than I did years ago. Who runs Telvin and what do they want from us?"

Eron shook his head, his pupils dilating and his nostrils flaring. "I never thought I'd see you again. I wanted it so much, and at the same time I prayed it would never happen."

Reaching up, I ran my hands through his short hair, pulling him forward. "Kiss me."

"I'm not the same as I was. None of what I've told you is a lie. I've been corrupted, and as much as I wish we could go back," he stepped away from me, his face twisting with regret, "we never can."

"We don't need to. I'm here. And you're here … alive. Nothing else matters for the moment."

"I don't know what's in store for us."

I touched his arm, needing contact. "All the more reason to take advantage of what could be our only chance."

Eron lifted his head, his gaze meeting mine once more. He stared at me a moment, his features drawn in a mask of neutrality … until he moved.

One moment I was on my feet, and the next I was on the bed, Eron covering me with his large body. Our lips and teeth clashed, desperation spurring both of us to act without tenderness of any kind. Eron was a part of my soul, my other half, and I needed him like I needed my next breath.

The cool air kissed my skin as Eron stripped my clothes from my body. When he plunged into me, I cried out, the pain of having gone so long without him, quickly morphing into pleasure.

Eron wasn't gentle as he pounded into me, one hard thrust after another. But I welcomed everything he had to give, scaling my nails down his back. Our bond roared to life, bright and shining within me, causing tears to trickle down my temples even as I cried out in pleasure.

You're my everything. I can never be without you again.

A kaleidoscope of colors exploded behind my eyes, and I quivered around Eron, wanting him to join me in my ecstasy. A few seconds later he did, a low growl accompanying his pulsating release inside of me.

For that one instant, all was right in my world.

"Fuck," he muttered, rolling off of me.

Blinking rapidly, I reached for Eron's retreating body. He stalked across the room, yanking white pants and a white T-shirt on with jerky movements. I instantly sensed his walls were back up, our bond severed again. My lower lip trembled. *What just happened? I thought I'd broken through all his barriers.*

"Eron," I said, my voice cracking. But the truth was, I didn't know what to say. Our Metza bond was still there, far beyond the walls Eron had built around himself. It was as strong as ever, and yet … yet, if I hadn't felt it, the way he was acting after just being intimate with me, would have made me doubt everything. Despite the nightmares, despite me knowing some of his darkest emotions regarding me.

Without looking at me, Eron spoke, "You clouded my judgment. That shouldn't have happened."

I opened and shut my mouth, wanting to argue with

him, but feeling ripped wide open. Instead, I decided to say nothing. Wrapping my arms around my middle, I rolled over, curling into myself.

I fell asleep like that, my mind slipping to happier times with Eron.

Chapter 11

Eron had been inside me, I'd felt our Metza bond ... *No.* I shook my head. I had to face the truth, the one I so desperately wanted to deny. Eron wasn't the same boy I'd fallen in love with. Of course, I wasn't the same girl he'd once known either. Years and circumstances had changed us. It was just that I'd always thought—

I choked back a sob. *No. I can't do this. I won't let this place break me again.* Or rather, since I'd never fully recovered from my last visit, I wouldn't let Telvin break me to the point of not being able to function.

Eron was a stranger to me now, despite our history, and despite our bond. He'd warned me, tried to make me see it, but I hadn't wanted to. *Now I do.* The Eron I knew might have been backed into a corner, he may have hurt me physically if he thought it would save my life in the long run, but he never would have fucked me and simply walked away. He never would have been so callous after such an intimacy.

So what did it mean? *Nothing.* Because regardless of Eron's feelings, or lack of them, I would always love him. I wasn't human, and I couldn't simply turn it all off. Maybe he discovered a way, but most likely he was simply broken beyond repair. I'd seen some of the things that had been done to him, the things he'd been forced to endure. *Which is my fault. If I wouldn't have left him here to rot—*

The door opened, revealing Eron, his gaze sliding over me warily. I hadn't moved from the bed, hadn't bothered getting dressed, I'd merely pulled a blanket around me like a cocoon.

He scowled, his voice rumbling low. "Why haven't you cleaned yourself? Gotten dressed? Why are you still there?"

I stared at him, having no idea what to say.

His boots echoed in the small room as he stomped across the floor, halting at the edge of the bed. "Did you hear me?"

I continued to stare, the urge to reach out and touch him rising within me. I couldn't seem to help myself. After all, it was Eron. I'd never be able to feel anything but love for him. I could try to convince myself that he was different, and yes, I could agree mentally, but my heart … my heart …

My lower lip trembled, and still, I remained silent.

"What's wrong with you?" He whipped his head around, searching the room, his eyes narrowed. "Was someone else here? Did they do something to you? Hurt you? Why aren't you speaking?"

I opened my mouth to tell him that he was the only one who could hurt me as deeply as I'd been injured. That no amount of physical torture could equal what he'd done to me emotionally. Instead, "Kiss me," tumbled from my lips. Apparently, my mind and heart had disconnected completely, determined to operate independently.

"No. It's what they want. It's why you're here."

I tilted my head, confusion setting in. "I'm here … to kiss you?"

Eron's nostrils flared. "No. You're here because they want more Mazatimz children, preferably Metzas like Xia and Tia. It's why—"

A buzzing sound had taken up residence in my head, the rest of what Eron said lost to me. Everything clicked into place. "How long have you known?"

"From the beginning."

"You said they wanted to test our bond. So you lied?"

"No. No, not completely. The things I told you, the things …" He sat, slumping onto the end of the bed, staring at the snake on his forearm. "I never lied. I simply omitted some truths."

Twisting the end of the blanket between my fingers, I swallowed around the lump in my throat. "So I was brought here to … breed?"

Eron snorted. "In a manner of speaking."

"And why didn't they make more Mazatimz children in the same manner Xia and Tia were created?"

"Because they're broken, or haven't you noticed? They thought maybe if we could have Metzas the old-fashioned way, then they'd have what they want."

"I don't understand." Or maybe I did. Maybe I didn't want to accept it—any of it. And didn't they know how truly rare Metzas were? Especially twins born as such. Eron and I could have twenty children, and none of them Metzas.

Eron shifted, his gaze boring into me even though I refused to meet it with my own. "Xia and Tia are now being groomed to be weapons, but that wasn't their original purpose. They want Metzas, powerful Metzas that they can use to heal on their command, at least for now. They kept me here because I could do procedures on their prisoners that others would kill in the process. Me, you … well, we've been their most important acquisitions ever. I'm stronger than any other Mazatimz they've acquired, even though you weren't here."

"So they took us to use our gifts, but then why did they let me escape? Why did they make me think you were dead?"

Eron pushed off the bed, pacing across the floor, back and forth, back and forth. "Because they were testing our bond. They wanted to push our limits, see what would happen. See how strong we were when separated. That part I didn't know. I was young and naïve, and I thought I could protect you. But this whole time they knew where you were, and eventually, no matter what I did, they were going to bring you back."

The Mazatimz gift was a coveted one. The power of healing was desired by all, and Telvin wouldn't be the first to attempt to control it through slavery of some sort. My people, because of our nature, had suffered countless attacks on our planet, which was why the security was so tight. *And yet not tight enough.* "They want to use Mazatimzs. Okay, I get that now. Definitely not surprising. But who are they? Who runs Telvin? What is their ultimate goal?"

Eron whirled around, his expression thunderous. "The Denards. They run everything."

A burst of laughter erupted from my chest. "I should have known. The Denards. I should have known. I mean, I knew Xia and Tia said they were important to the Denards, but … I should have known they ran everything. I thought maybe the Denards had hired Telvin or … I don't know, but I should have figured."

It seemed as if the Denards were behind every heinous act I came across lately. From infecting the Gartians with the G-Pox to attempting to eradicate the phoenix species. The Denards were cruel and sadistic, with the only clear goal being power over everyone and everything within their reach. When had their species come into existence, and how long had they been a blight on the Universe? *Jane and Ash are right. We have to stop them no matter the cost.*

"What?" I muttered. Eron had been speaking again, but I'd been lost in my own thoughts.

He stalked over to stand directly in front of me, his hands covering my shoulders. "When they told me that I had to impregnate you, of course I said no. I could never —would never—not like that." His fingers dug into my flesh painfully. "That's when they decided to motivate me by torturing you ..."

Our gazes clashed, understanding dawning. What the twins had been doing, what Eron had unwillingly done, all of it had been to force his hand. And I'd unknowingly played right into it when I'd given myself to him. Sure, he'd been naked in front of me, but— "Why didn't you say something? Why didn't you say no? Why the hell did you parade around in front of me in nothing but a towel?"

"I wanted them to think I was attempting to seduce you." He let me go, his arms falling at his sides as he dropped his head, shame rolling off of him in palpable waves. "But I was weak. I wanted ... want you. I've never stopped, never for one second stopped—" His voice cracked, cutting him off. "Everything I've done since I first stepped into this place has been weak, everything except one thing."

Standing, I rushed to him, dragging the sheet with me, and threw my arms around his waist. I knew what that one thing was. He'd done Telvin's bidding to keep me safe, or at least that's what he thought he was doing. "It's okay. It'll be—"

"No." He shoved me away from him. "None of it will be okay. Don't you get it? They want me to impregnate you, and yeah, the means to that end ... fuck. I want it. I want you any way I can have you, but ... They'll take our children. They'll take them from us."

"Or they'll torture me."

"Yes. Or they'll torture you."

Eron was right. Both choices would end in one agony or another. *We have to find a way out of here. Now.* "You said before that you were getting me out of here, what about you? Is there a way to get both of us out?"

"Things have changed, or I guess I know the truth of things. I'm still able to walk around relatively unsupervised, but my access to certain parts of Telvin has been revoked. They've closed off all escape routes."

I gnawed on the inside of my cheek, considering. "We have to get a message to my crew on the Pittsburgh. They have resources. They can get us out of here." I was worried that they hadn't shown up already. I had no idea if they'd be able to find Telvin on their own. Masha and Dar had seemed confident about tracing the pod Xia and Tia had arrived in, but since they'd been sent to infiltrate The Pittsburgh and bring me back, the coordinates had surely been tampered with. What if they were chasing down false lead after false lead? I couldn't count on them to save us, but getting a message to them wouldn't hurt.

"You don't want to bring your crew here. Not if you care about them at all. I've heard talk. Your captain, Jane, she's part phoenix, isn't she?"

"Yes, she's a spliced human."

"They'd love to get their hands on someone like her, to cut her open and see what makes her tick. There would be no mercy for someone like her."

I knew the history of the Denards with the phoenix,

even with Jane personally. I couldn't risk bringing them to Telvin under those circumstances. "Okay, we'll find another way." Eron's mouth pressed into a flat line, his eyes dulling. "We will. I promise."

"And until then?"

"We'll do what we need to survive."

Chapter 12

Being in Telvin did funny things to my concept of time. The nature of such a place brought out heightened emotions, and sped along things that needed time and space to develop. For example, my and Eron's relationship. When we'd first been reunited, he'd been cold, distant, and a stranger on a multitude of levels. Within a matter of days, or maybe even hours, I'd managed to find a crack in his armor. Soon, he was divulging his feelings and secrets. He was telling me things that I knew would have taken months, if not years, to reveal if we were anywhere else. Maybe some of it had to do with our Metza bond, but that was only a part of it.

Metzas were drawn to each other, but often nothing more than a close friendship developed. Eron and I shared love, the kind that all species with a soul dreamt about. And we'd been separated for so long. Both of us yearned for what we used to share. Not only had he been the boy I loved, but he had always been my best friend since the moment I became conscious of my world.

A flip had been switched in Eron, and although remorse and shame still clung to him, I once again felt optimistic about my ability to ultimately heal him—to heal us. After all, we were Mazatimzs, and Metzas at that. We could handle anything, as long as we were together.

"So they just expect us to breed, like animals?" I bit my lower lip, studying Eron's profile.

Telvin's latest tactic was to confine both of us to Eron's living quarters, stripped of all our clothing. Food and drink were delivered regularly through a newly revealed slot near the main door. I suspected some kind of sexual mood enhancer in our refreshments if my constant state of arousal was any indication, not to mention Eron's. It was beginning to fog my brain, clouding my judgment. I needed to be concentrating on an escape plan, but instead, my efforts were focused on not gazing with hunger at Eron's sculpted body, and massive erection. *Eyes up. Keep your damn eyes up.*

"I don't know how much longer I can withstand this," Eron muttered, shifting uncomfortably. His fists balled up at his sides in an effort not to touch himself, or me. Both would be bad. If he touched himself, then I wouldn't be far behind, just imagining his fist stroking along …

I bit the inside of my cheek, my breath coming out in short little spurts, my pulse pounding between my legs. "At least torture is temporarily off the table."

"This is its own brand of torture."

I swallowed in an attempt to return saliva to my mouth. "Maybe we should just—"

"No."

"I won't get pregnant right away. I mean, if we just—"

"No."

"Even if I do get pregnant, that'll buy us time. They'll have to wait until I give birth."

Eron's eyes were fierce when they met mine. "You don't know if they plan to let you carry it. And you can be damn sure the moment you're with child, they'll separate us again."

He was right. It all made sense. I knew it, but … "We could do other things." *I swear if I get out of here in one piece, I will never mock Jane for letting her hormones make decisions for her again.*

"It won't be enough, and we both know it."

"Then we have to stop eating. Maybe then—"

Eron tilted his head. "Why?"

"The drugs of course. It's what's making us like this." I waved my arms at him and then myself in annoyance. "If we stop taking the drugs then it'll be easier. We'll just have a different kind of hunger." I snorted, hating how ridiculous I sounded. Mazatimzs experienced sexual arousal similar to humans, but not on the same level. Humans were known—even spliced humans, since purebred humans no longer existed—to be a sexually driven species. Very few in the Universe rivaled them. I had a feeling Eron and I did currently. My brain was addled with nothing but thoughts of sex.

"There were no drugs in our food or drink."

I flicked my gaze up to meet Eron's. My cheeks heated when I realized my gaze had drifted down to his erection. "What? Um, what did you say?"

"I said there were no drugs in our food or drink. Where did you get that idea?"

"Of course there were. Why do you think there wasn't?"

"Because I know there weren't any drugs in them. They wouldn't want to tamper with the children they hope we produce. They won't give you any more drugs of any kind."

Recoiling, my jaw slackened with surprise. Eron would know better than I would the inner workings of Telvin. If he didn't think they would put some kind of sexual enhancers in our food, then they probably hadn't. Which meant …

I brought my legs up to my chest, squeezing my eyes shut. *What I'm feeling for him, and what he's feeling for me is all us.* I kept reminding myself of the differences between Mazatimzs and humans, and comparing myself to Jane, always considering my species better, humans lacking in so many ways. *Maybe we're not so different after all. Maybe we're just as bigoted as the Denards are in our own way.*

It was no secret the Universe considered any species with human DNA to be sub-par in practically every way. I'd grown to love Jane like a sister but still considered her overly emotional, sex-driven, reckless—I shook my head. I hadn't been fair. I'd considered Mazatimzs a superior species, and every time I did something I didn't approve of on some level, I dissected it against what Jane would do. *Maybe none of us are so different after all.*

"I'm sorry, Eron, I've been so stupid about everything."

Eron cleared his throat, his finger tracing the snake tattoo on his forearm. "We were sheltered our whole lives before we were brought here. We didn't know what it was really like beyond the boundaries of our own little society. Both of us did the best we could."

I shifted, stretching my legs out in front of me, my toes almost touching his hip. "You keep saying that we did our best, but I see the way you're looking at your snake tattoo, and I haven't forgotten so easily what you told me about its meaning. You obviously don't believe you did your best. Don't lie to me. Not anymore."

Eron nodded, his gaze remaining fixated on his arm. "You're right. I don't believe I did my best. Not with anything." His fist clenched tighter, the veins in his arm popping out. "I should have been able to protect you at the very least. I should never have let you be taken—us be taken. I should have learned to fight. I should have—" He dropped his head into his hands, his voice muffled. "I should have done whatever necessary to protect you. This whole time I thought that's what I was doing, and I was wrong. So wrong."

Rising to my knees, I crept across the bed, leaning into his back and wrapping my arms around his shoulders. "You said it yourself. We were young, and we were sheltered. We had no idea how to protect ourselves. The responsibility didn't fall solely on you. I left you here …" Tears filled my eyes and spilled down my face, running off my chin onto Eron's back.

"I'm broken, Tamzy, more than you know." One of his hands moved up to cover mine. "I-I'm glad you're here. Despite what it means, what you've already suffered, and what you're going to suffer, I'm glad you're here. And I should never under any circumstances feel that way. I shouldn't … I just shouldn't."

My heart twisted and bled. He was right. He was more broken than I could fathom, but I understood. He thought it tainted him in some manner to feel that way, but he couldn't help it. I pressed my lips to the back of his neck, whispering against it, "You're a good male, Eron. You've merely been forced into horrible situations."

He leaned into me, sighing heavily. "You always see the good in every creature, even if the bad outweighs it."

"No. The bad could never outweigh the good in you. Never." As if they had a mind of their own, my hands slid down his chest, tracing the contours of his muscles. My breath fanned across his neck, drawing a shiver from him. I knew I should stop, and back away before things progressed, but I was compelled to comfort Eron any way I knew how.

I leaned in, kissing along his shoulders. "You know, the snake symbolizes transmutation in some cultures. The mark on your arm, it doesn't have to mean what it did before, if you don't want it to."

Eron shifted, turning so I could kiss along the side of

his neck, his eyes closed in supplication. "What cultures are these?"

"Mmm … I read about them in an Earth book once."

"Transmutation of what exactly?" Eron's fingers twisted in my hair, his mouth sliding along my jaw.

"Make the bad into good. I'll help you. We can do anything together."

"Us. Together. Yeah."

His lips sealed over my mouth, his tongue plunging in to dominate completely, although I gave him control willingly. His taste was familiar, yet exhilarating, the energy between us, our bond, crackled audibly in the air.

Eron yanked away from me abruptly, his pupils blown, and expression wild. "We can't. I want it, so fucking much, but we can't."

I nodded, but something inside of me had snapped. *Fuck it.* Jumping off the bed, I swung around to get in front of Eron, shoving him back. Before he could react, I straddled his thighs, leaning forward to capture his wrists, pressing them into the mattress.

"What are you doing?" he demanded.

"I need you, Eron, and I refuse to let them dictate our lives for one second longer. We have a choice. There's always a choice. And I choose you, whatever that means. It's us together."

Eron bucked halfheartedly underneath me. He wanted me just as much as I wanted him, but he was afraid. "They'll take our—"

"No. We won't let them. We're going to get out of

here." Ever since the day we'd been taken, I'd been allowing fear to run my life. Even when I'd escaped and been on The Pittsburgh where I thought I'd been safe, fear had been my constant companion. It was time for me to transmute some things of my own.

I ground my hips down, sliding against Eron's cock, my entire body trembling with anticipation. "I love you," I murmured.

That was all it took. Eron lifted up, plunging into me with ease, since I was already ready and willing. I undulated in a slow rhythm, throwing my head back as I grabbed his thighs for leverage. Rocking up and down, I took my time, wanting to savor every second of us being together.

Eron's hands covered my breasts, squeezing and kneading, before trailing down to encircle my waist. I leaned forward, meeting his gaze briefly, and then captured his lips with mine. He grabbed my ass, lifting me up so he could pivot against me with more force. Moaning, I let him take control, losing myself in him completely.

My muscles coiled tight, the energy from our bond zinging through my system, lighting every nerve ending on fire.

And then I fell to pieces, smashed apart by pure pleasure. Eron was right there with me, our souls twining together through our bond, a closeness to him I hadn't felt since before we were taken. It was pure joy, more than physically, but a euphoria brought on by complete bliss of the metaphysical kind blended with perfect sexual compatibility.

The metal door to the room slammed open, and I screamed reflexively, scrambling to cover myself. A familiar voice, filled with sarcasm, met my ears. I whirled around, a sheet clutched to my chest. Standing there, in all of her Steampunk, Earth-obsessed glory, was Jane, a smirk adorning her face, and a laser gun clutched in her hand.

"What? How?" I shook my head. It didn't matter. Plus, without my translator implants, I wouldn't be able to understand her answer.

Eron wrapped a blanket around his waist and stood to help secure the sheet in a manageable way around my body. Jane said something else, and I shook my head, but before I could say anything, Eron responded for me. "Her translator implants were removed. For the time being, I'll have to translate what you say to her."

Jane snorted, saying something ladened with annoyance, and of course more sarcasm. Narrowing my eyes at her, I snapped, "Shut up. Whatever you said, I don't like it." She laughed, quirking an eyebrow at me, and then glanced suggestively at Eron. "We don't have time for this," I huffed. Sure, me being the naked one found in a compromising situation was new, and I was positive I'd never hear the end of it.

Jane rolled her eyes, said a few sentences, and disappeared into the hallway.

"She said to follow her, and to not worry, she has everything under control."

I groaned, my feelings of relief fizzling. Tension hastened my strides out the door. I hadn't been worried until Jane said she had everything under control. It was code for her winging it and hoping for the best. I didn't need to actually hear her say that much to know exactly what she meant—nothing was lost in that translation.

I grabbed Eron's hand, tugging him after me. "Come on, we need to hurry before everything goes to shit. Again."

Chapter 13

"Which way did she go?" I panted, my chest heaving from exertion.

Eron tilted his head, listening. "That way." He pointed to the right. "I hear a commotion, and I assume Jane is the cause of it."

"Isn't she always?" I muttered, staggering to the right, forcing my body to move faster than it wanted to at the moment.

Loud foot tread caught my attention and I pulled up short, not wanting to run headlong into anyone who would attempt to stop us from escaping. Jane sped around the corner, making her way past us with a few angry words.

"She went the wrong way apparently," Eron said.

"Of course she did." Our bare feet pounded against the cool metal floors as we sprinted after her, my nerves ratcheting up a few levels. How did Jane get into Telvin to find us when she clearly didn't have a clue about how to find her way out? *If she wings every mission like this, it's a miracle she snags as many bounties as she does.*

At the end of the corridor, Jane squared off with the creature. Her laser gun lay on the floor between them, a few scorch marks on the ceiling and walls. Flames burned in her palms, flickering and casting shadows around her. The creature wore a fierce expression, not even the slightest bit intimidated by Jane's phoenix abilities. I was riveted in place, scarcely breathing. *What if Jane doesn't win this battle?*

Eron grabbed my arm, spinning me around. "Let's go. We can use the distraction as a chance to escape."

I slapped at his hand. "Wait. We can't just leave Jane here."

"She'll be able to handle herself." Without another word, he slung me over his shoulder.

"No. We don't know that. Put me down. Eron, put me down." His shoulder dug into my stomach, causing nausea to roll through me as I was jostled around. "Eron … please." I couldn't leave Jane behind not knowing if she in fact had things under control. What if she got herself captured because of me? I'd never be able to live with myself. But Eron didn't have the same concerns.

Heading in the opposite direction we came from, Eron continued carrying me until we reached an area of Telvin I'd never seen before, where he placed me gently on my feet. We were in a small cargo bay, several miniature escape pods lined up, open, and ready to launch. They were cylindrical and skinny, each of them having one seat in the center. It appeared as if the pilot was supposed to stand. I'd never seen such a design before, although it did remind me a bit of the pod Jane had used to flee from Ambassador Aralias' ship.

Eron crouched down next to what looked like a central control pad of some sort, going to work.

"If you knew this was here, then why didn't you tell Jane?"

"Because I was hoping to make our getaway in a ship. These pods are difficult to control and easy to apprehend. Beggars can't be choosers, though."

I nibbled my bottom lip. "It'll be fine. We can head towards The Pittsburgh, it's somewhere close or Jane wouldn't be here." I wasn't sure who I was trying to convince though, Eron or myself.

A deafening buzzer came to life, accompanied by flashing lights. I glanced down at Eron who was grimacing as he pried a metal panel open, tearing at wires. He stood a second later, and scooped me up, placing me into the nearest pod, clambering in after me. It was a tight squeeze, but still manageable. He yanked the door closed and strapped us in, although the flimsy material for the harnesses made them nothing more than ornamental. There were no windows, but a navigation grid lit up just above the controls, along with steering panels.

"Hold on, this is going to be a bumpy ride."

I glanced around, noting the walls were smooth with no handles or grooves. "Hold on to what?" I squeaked.

"Me." Eron's lips brushed across mine briefly, his energy snapping along my skin. Pulling away, he grinned, his eyes twinkling for the first time since we'd been separated all those years ago, both of his dimples set deeply in his cheeks.

Before I had time to consider what it meant or to process anything, the engine roared to life, propelling us forward, and plastering me against the seat. I stared at Eron's profile, his countenance fixed in concentration as he steered.

"Why didn't you ever use one of these to escape yourself?" It didn't make sense. He could have left at any time.

"I told you. I had to stay to protect you."

"You could have left … found me."

His jaw muscles feathered, his gaze flickering to me. "And if I didn't find you? I'd have wondered if they replaced me with you. I couldn't risk it."

So many mistakes were made on both our parts. It wasn't a new thought, but one I couldn't let go of. Eron and I had been so young, so little known about the Universe outside of our sheltered lives. Eron did what he thought he had to do to protect me, sacrificing himself completely. The guilt of it ate at me like nothing else could. *Will I ever be able to move past this?*

"Don't," he growled. "I feel your guilt, and I don't want you to think that way. It was my choice. And I'd do it again if it meant keeping you safe. I'd do anything to keep you safe."

Something dark sparked through our bond—not guilt like I was subjecting myself to—and it sank into my chest, constricting like a steel band around my lungs. *What's going on in that head of yours?* Eron was far from healed emotionally, and I knew what I'd felt from him would be the first of many things I'd have to help him with, whatever it was.

The pod banked sharply to the left, cutting off my intended words. I slid back, bracing myself as best as I could, trying not to interfere with Eron's mobility. He was the one flying after all. With such a tight fit, the confined space began to warm with our body heat quickly. Sweat dribbled down my spine, and my palms slipped along the wall. I pushed my toes against the front of the pod, but without shoes, it didn't do much good as far as keeping me in place.

"There's a ship nearby," Eron muttered. "I hope it's The Pittsburgh because I can't get a read on the make from here."

"There isn't any way to contact them?"

"No. These pods are backups, they don't even have spare oxygen."

"If it's The Pittsburgh, they'll—"

The pod jerked, slamming both of us against the seat. Eron punched a few buttons, his hands falling to his sides a second later. "We're locked in a tractor beam."

I nodded, slipping my hand in his, and leaning my head against his chest. "Which was what I was going to say … if it's them, they'll yank us in on a tractor beam." I exhaled a sigh of relief. As soon as we were on the ship, and Jane made her way back, everything would be fine. After all the years I'd pined over Eron's loss, I'd have him with me on The Pittsburgh. It seemed almost too good to be true.

Eron's arm worked its way under me, wrapping around my waist. He twisted to the side so we were facing each other instead of side by side. The sheet I was wearing was plastered to my skin with sweat, as was his towel. It left very little to the imagination.

"I love you, Tamzy, and I would do anything to keep you safe. Your life is more important than mine. Always remember that."

I scrunched my nose up. "I won't need to anymore. We're safe. Or we will be soon."

Rocking up on my tiptoes, I kissed him, groaning with delight the moment my tongue flicked against his. Eron fisted my hair, pressing the length of his body into mine, his pelvis pivoting in a circular motion, wrenching another moan from my throat.

How did I survive without this? I had to have known on some level that he was still alive. Those thoughts sobered me quickly, and I pulled away from Eron's embrace as much as our limited space allowed me. *Was I out there, knowingly living my life while he rotted in Telvin?*

Eron cupped the side of my face, forcing my gaze up to his. "Enough with the guilt."

"I had to have known on some level that you were alive

… and I just left you there." My vision blurred as tears gathered in the corners of my eyes.

"No. I shut myself off from you, remember? There was no way you could have felt me through our bond."

"And yet I never felt your death. Shouldn't I have realized that?" Not to mention the nightmares …

Eron swiped at a tear as it trailed down my cheek. "I'm not sure it would have felt any different."

I took in a shuddering breath. "Maybe." The pod clanged to a stop. Swallowing, I forced a smile. "I guess none of it matters now." Which I wished was true. But Eron wasn't the only one who was going to need time to unpack his baggage.

We fell into silence waiting for the pod to be opened. Without windows, it would have been too risky to exit without knowing what was going on. With a whirl and hum, the door unlocked, lifting from the outside. Dar was the first face I saw, his dark gaze darting over us warily before relaxing. Behind him stood Masha, a grin spreading across her face when our eyes met. She said something I didn't understand.

"We're not injured," Eron responded.

Zula stepped into my line of sight. Her words and tone were curt and filled with worry.

Eron rolled to the side, and pulled himself from the pod, offering his hand to me. Grabbing it, I awkwardly found my own footing. "Jane shouldn't be too far behind us. I hope," I said, guessing what Zula had asked about.

Crossing her arms over her chest, Zula's lips pressed

into a thin line. More words I couldn't understand spilled from her mouth.

I shook my head. "I need to get some new translator implants installed before we can have this or any kind of conversation. I don't have a clue what any of you are saying except for Eron."

Zula addressed Eron, and he squeezed my hand, responding to Zula, "Yes, they removed her implants. But all of her other injuries are healed."

Relief played across Zula's blue-tinged face, and she nodded, moving out of the way. On shaky legs, I led Eron out of the airlock and through The Pittsburgh, heading straight for the medical wing.

I kept extra translator implants in stock as a rule, never knowing when one of the crew could potentially damage one of theirs, specifically Jane. As a bounty hunter, she was rough on everything, even her own body.

I pulled the tray of packaged translators from my main storage locker and readied them for insertion. "I'm going to need your help with these. I could put them in myself if I had to, but …"

I glanced up as Eron took the package from my hand. "But you don't have to do everything yourself now that I'm here."

And there it was. I'd found a family among the crew of The Pittsburgh. Jane, Zula, and Masha were sisters of my heart. But underneath it all, the hole Eron had left in my heart caused an isolation of my soul. Nothing except Eron himself could fill such a gap within me.

I leaned into him, the spattering of his lavender chest hair abrading my cheek as I rubbed against him. It was as if I could breathe fully for the first time in years.

Everything is going to be fine now. Better than fine. Because we're together again. And together we can handle anything.

Chapter 14

I'd fallen asleep shortly after Eron inserted my translators, partly from exhaustion, both physical and mental, and the rest from an added push from Eron's abilities. He knew I needed a deep healing sleep before I took on the world again. I had to regroup and re-energize, or I wouldn't be any good to anyone.

I didn't have any dreams I could remember, but I awoke with a deep-seated feeling of dread. *Something's wrong.* Eron was curled around my back, his face flush with my neck, his legs entangled with mine, and one strong arm possessively draped over my middle. Careful not to disturb him, I glanced around my living quarters. Everything was seemingly in place. No sounds out of the ordinary alerted me to any potential problems either. Forcing myself to relax, I snuggled back into Eron, my eyelids drooping from their sudden weight. *You're being paranoid, which is to be expected after being in Telvin again.* Sleep overtook me once more.

I jerked awake, instantly aware that I was alone, not sure how much time had passed. Rubbing my sleep-encrusted eyes, I stumbled from bed, lured by the tether of energy that bound me to Eron. I paused before exiting my quarters to pull some clothes on, realizing I was naked, the sheet I'd been wearing pooled on the floor alongside the bed.

Once dressed, I clomped through the corridors, zeroing in on Eron. When I found him, he was hunched over the escape pod we'd arrived in, fiddling with something I couldn't see. He wore black pants and a matching top, much like mine, but his were sized to fit his much larger body. A smile played across my lips at how right he looked being on The Pittsburgh.

I leaned against the wall, admiring his arm and shoulder muscles, and the way they moved and bunched as he worked. "What are you doing?"

He didn't lift his head or so much as spare me a glance. "Attempting to install a better navigation system in this thing."

"Why?"

"You never know when we might need it."

Scowling, I shuffled closer. "We won't need it. Jane will probably want to sell it for parts or to someone who might have use for it."

"It's ours. She can't do that."

Placing a hand on his shoulder, I squeezed

reassuringly. "We won't need it, and it's Jane's right to sell it. I work on her ship as a healer. She provides food, shelter, and—"

"You want to stay here?" Eron rose, his gaze searching mine.

"Where else would we go? Plus, Jane, Zula, and Masha, they're like family to me now. It's where I've made a life for myself over the past decade." I wrapped my arms around his waist, staring up at him.

"I thought you'd want to start fresh somewhere … with me."

I'd never even considered being anywhere else. I'd just assumed Eron would fit in flawlessly with my life. Maybe I was being unfair. It was just the thought of not being part of the crew on The Pittsburgh twisted my insides, even if I was with Eron somewhere else. I wanted both. "We could be happy here."

"It's not safe for us here."

"What's that supposed to mean?" His emotions were in turmoil and completely indecipherable.

"Telvin knew exactly where you were the entire time. They could—"

"How? I never asked. How did they know? There's no tracker implanted inside me, and The Pittsburgh isn't easily—"

"Xia and Tia."

Their names hung in the air between us, dark and thick. I didn't want to think about them, had forced my mind to steer away every time it had the urge to dredge up questions. They were technically my children, but I wanted no part in their lives. I contributed to their DNA, but not to their souls, if they even had any.

My fingers dug into the muscular expanse of Eron's back, and he tightened his grip around me in response. "But that means they can still find me … us."

"Which is why it's not safe here." Eron pulled away from me, hunching over the pod once more.

"But it won't be safe anywhere. It's actually safer here because we'll constantly be on the move. The only better place would be …" I couldn't even say the words. I never wanted to go back to our home planet, it was another subject I didn't let my mind wander to. I carefully kept myself from even thinking its name … ever. Even now, having Eron back, that place held too many memories I could never face.

"I'm formulating a plan."

I quirked a brow. "Really? Are you going to share?" Silence fell over us, Eron ignoring me in favor of his work on the pod. I expelled an exasperated breath. "Well, I'm going to go talk to Zula, and check in on Jane." I didn't know for sure, but I was assuming Jane was back from Telvin. Otherwise, Zula would have flown into a panic by now, sending the entire ship into a tizzy.

Eron grunted as his only response. I sighed again demonstratively, knowing it was overkill since he surely felt my annoyance through our bond as well. I stomped away, grumbling under my breath, "Maybe Jane has it right. Maybe being bonded to a male of any species drives females to drink."

It wasn't just Eron's lack of communication skills that was getting under my skin. I had no idea what was going on with him. He continued to be hot and cold with me, leaving me to feel safe and content one moment, and like he was practically a stranger the next. I understood that he'd been traumatized in Telvin, I'd seen some of his memories, but it would be nice if he at least pretended to try with me.

Grimacing, I internally chastised myself. *Stop. You're not being fair. You don't know all the things he's been through. You've only seen a few fragments while you slept. You have no idea what experiencing those things firsthand has done to him, plus all the rest. Give him time. Time will heal all his wounds. You can't expect him to be the way he was before. Love him for who he is now.*

"Tamzea!" Jane appeared as if from nowhere, crushing me in an uncharacteristic hug. "I was just coming to find you."

Flitting my hands around, I assessed her energy levels, searching for any injuries. "What happened back there? Are you hurt?"

"Psst … half phoenix badass here. I'm fine."

"Good. I was worried." Grinning, I tapped behind my right ear. "I can understand you again. And you really need to explain to me how you found us and got into Telvin to begin with. Seriously. The way you showed up like that was … shocking." I didn't want to encourage talk of how she'd found us, but my curiosity regarding her antics was too great to be denied.

Jane stepped away from me, her face pinched with worry. "Later. I'll explain everything later. Have you seen Zula?"

"Umm ... no. Not since I got back on the ship. But I've been preoccupied. Why?"

Jane crossed her arms over her chest, eyes narrowed in thought. "I managed to grab one of those pods to escape, my transport cut off from me. Zula brought me in, said she was coming right back, and now I can't find her."

"Huh. Well, she has to be around here somewhere. After all, we are on a ship out in space."

"And Nina, I haven't seen her either."

Why was Jane so worried? Did she know something I didn't? As small as The Pittsburgh was, it sometimes felt cavernous at times for how often people seemed to go missing. It was usually because they didn't want to be found, though. "Well, you know Nina, she's probably skulking around in the shadows somewhere." My mind immediately went to how she'd tried to talk to me right before I'd been abducted by Xia and Tia. How had she known, and if she had, why didn't she do anything?

I leaned towards the ship's intercom, pressing the button down. "Zula, Nina, can you please let Jane know where you are? Thank you."

Jane snorted. "Right. That would have been so much easier. Oops. It's been a long day." Her boot rapped against the floor as we waited. "What's taking so long?" Ever the impatient one, Jane moved over to press down the intercom button herself, yelling into the speaker, "Hey! Zula! Nina! Any time now!"

Dar rounded the corner, pausing behind Jane, his head tilting with curiosity. "Why are the two of you standing out here?" His gaze flitted around the corridor as if he would be clued in by something there.

Jane rolled her eyes, motioning to the intercom. "Didn't you just hear me calling for Zula and Nina? We're obviously waiting for a response of some kind. And seriously, what the hell is taking them so long?" She smashed down the intercom button again. "Hello! Zula! Nina! Where the hell are the two of you?"

"Maybe the intercom isn't working in the entire ship," I suggested, pushing down my unease. *Something isn't right.*

Dar shook his head. "No. Masha just ran a systems check about an hour ago. Some of the outlets were damaged so she repaired them, and made sure everything was integrated into the system."

Jane's nostrils flared. "This isn't like Zula."

"I agree, but maybe—"

"Masha!" Dar pushed past Jane, shoving her into the wall. I jumped to the side, narrowly avoiding a collision.

Between Zula and Nina not responding to Jane, and Dar's panic, I knew my gut had been right, something was very wrong. Jane and I sped after Dar, losing sight of him several times as he dashed past the engine room, and headed straight for the center of the ship.

Just as I was about to enter the control room hot on

Jane and Dar's heels, a hand clamped over my mouth, and an arm wrapped around my waist. My startled scream was muffled as I was dragged backwards.

"Shhh," Eron rumbled in my ear. I immediately stopped struggling, although I was still unsure of what was going on. "Good. We're getting out of here now."

My mind reeled. He couldn't mean what I thought he meant. I shook my head, yanking on his hand. "No. We can't leave. We—"

"This ship is about to be crawling with Denards. Even though I made a deal to keep us safe, I'm not stupid enough to trust their word again. We're not going to be here by the time they arrive."

My heart dropped into my stomach. "What did you do?"

"I told you I'd do whatever it took to keep you safe."

"Oh, Eron, no. What did you do?" Dread rolled over me, pulling me into a dark abyss.

"I told you. I won't let anything happen to you again."

"We have to warn Jane." Wrenching away from Eron, I scurried for the ladder, panic making me quick.

But Eron was quicker. His arms slid around my mouth and waist again, and he yanked me against his chest. "We don't have a choice."

Tearing at his hand with my teeth, I screamed, but his fingers pressed into my cheeks, holding tight. *I have to warn Jane. I can't let something happen to my friends because of me. I can't let this happen.* I kicked and bit, using all of my strength to fight the male I loved, and the one who just betrayed me.

"I'm sorry," Eron whispered.

My vision faltered, my energy sucked away from me through our bond. He was using the same technique Xia and Tia had used, although he had a bit more finesse and control.

"I'll never forgive you," I hissed, sagging against him. "Never."

"Your hate I can live with, but at least you'll be safe." He hoisted me into his arms, cradling my limp form against his chest. "This was the only way."

As I slipped into unconsciousness, my mind rifled through the things that had led us to this moment—the moment where Eron truly betrayed me. I'd trusted him completely, and he'd used it against me. It was crystal clear to me now. We'd been allowed to escape, placing Eron in the optimal position to sabotage The Pittsburgh from the inside. He was no better than Xia and Tia. All of them had been tainted by Telvin, and in many ways, so had I.

I'll figure out a way to fix it. All of it. Somehow.

Chapter 15

My world was awash in confusion. Bits of color and pieces of information swirled around me. The shrill sound of an alarm. Angry voices. The underside of Eron's jawline. The scent of something burning. A cold surface under my cheek. Everything was a clue to what was happening, but I couldn't fight past the exhaustion holding my body hostage to fit the puzzle together.

Turmoil slithered down my bond from Eron, encasing me in black emotions—fear, desperation, and regret. I wanted to soothe him, fix what was wrong, if only I could figure out what exactly that was.

Everything faded to a dull grey, and I hovered there, memories of Eron and me together coming in flashes.

"I saved her." Eron grinned, hugging the infant alien in his arms. It was green with scales, reptilian in nature, its eyes huge and luminous as it gazed up at its savior.

Rising onto my tiptoes, I kissed his cheek. "Of course you did. Now we just have to find her family."

A small frown formed on his lips. "I wish I could save them all."

"I know. Me too. But remember, it's impossible. We do what we can, and we have to let that be enough."

As part of our training, our parents allowed us to travel with Mazatimz envoys to planets in need of medical aid. We would heal as many as we could before our energy was depleted to the point of danger. Oftentimes the trips were emotionally, as well as physically, draining. Not being able to save every being in need of help was a knife twisted in our Mazatimz hearts. It was part of who we were to want to heal every last soul, even if it killed us. Learning to control that urge was one of the most important parts of our training. And the most difficult. If we didn't learn, it would eventually kill us.

Brushing my hand over the alien child in Eron's arms, I smiled. "It'll never be enough for us. But it was enough for her. You saved her—you saved her whole world."

Eron nodded. "You're right, I know you are, but I just wish—"

The memory morphed into another.

Dropping to the floor, uncontrollable sobs wracked my body. I was so powerful, but I hadn't been able to save him. His body was past the point of repair, even when I drew on my Metza bond, nearly depleting Eron of his energy as well.

Strong arms encircled me. "You did all you could," Eron murmured into my hair.

"He was just a child. Why would anyone do such a thing? Why?"

The boy on the table had been part human and part wolf shifter, the combination not blending well, leaving him more animal than anything. Apparently, someone had taken offense and beaten him to the point of death. I'd tried to heal him, but he'd been brought to me too late. He couldn't have been older than six in human years.

"It's not fair," I sobbed. "How could anyone be so cruel?"

"It's not in our nature to understand. Our species isn't capable of such horrors. Not unless broken. You know this."

It was true. I did know, intellectually, but my heart ... my heart couldn't accept it. "He was just a child." My lungs burned as I gasped for breath. "He didn't do anything wrong."

"Shhh ... It'll be okay. I have you. Hold onto me."

The memory shifted, colors and shapes wavering to form another image.

"Listen to me," Eron whispered in my ear, goose bumps erupting across my flesh. "I will get you out of here somehow. That's all I can promise anymore. Nothing else. Forget who I was before, the things I swore to you. Because there's no hope for me. I made peace with that fact a long time ago."

"No, I don't accept that. I won't leave here without you again. Before I thought you were dead. I—"

"You're here for a reason. The twins are growing and maturing, and they want to understand their capabilities. But they're too important to test. That's why you're here. They want to test both of us. They think I haven't figured it out yet, but I

know they feel my usefulness has reached its expiration date without you. Once I get you out of here, they will kill me."

"Then we'll both get out of here."

"You wouldn't say that if you truly understood what I've become—the things I've done. You should hate me."

I opened my eyes, tears running down my temples into my hair. Eron had been trying to tell me, but I wouldn't listen. His time at Telvin had broken him completely. He wasn't the same boy I'd fallen in love with, he was a shattered male who I couldn't trust. *But he let himself be broken for you.*

"Tamzea."

Tilting my head to the side, I met Jane's gaze. She was perched in a chair beside my bed. Everything came flooding back to me, Eron, the Denards … my heart took off at a gallop.

"What happened?" I croaked. "Where's Eron?"

Jane's expression hardened, her pupils erupting in flames. "We nearly didn't make it out of that one. Thank God for that Gartian cloaking device or we would all be toast by now. As it is, Zula, Masha, and Nina … Telvin has them."

Fear iced my veins. "How?" But I already knew. *Eron.*

"You're lucky Dar didn't kill him. I had half a mind to do it myself." Jane rocked back, her chair balancing on two legs. "But I was afraid it would affect you somehow. So instead I threw him in a cell."

"Jane, he's … I—" Swallowing, I turned away. My first instinct was to defend Eron, but what he'd done was unforgivable. I understood why he'd betrayed me, surprisingly I even got that he thought he was protecting me, but none of that made what he'd done okay.

Jane touched my arm, her skin hot. "I get it. Okay? I do. I can't even imagine the kind of hell he's been living in. And he loves you. Even that much is clear to me. But, Tamzea, he fucked us over."

"I know," I rasped, my throat raw with emotion. "And I'm sorry. It's all my fault."

"Whoa, whoa, whoa, whoa, whoa. Hold on there. None of this is your fault. Why would you think that?"

I sniffled. "I see the good in everyone. I want to heal and forgive, soothe and protect. I thought I could heal him. I thought that underneath the pain was the old Eron. None of this would have happened if I was more like you. If I just—"

"Stop right there. Now, you listen very carefully to what I'm about to say. Yes, you want to heal and protect everyone. You don't handle stressful situations, aside from the bloody kind, very well. But that doesn't make you weak or a liability of any kind. Your strength is different than mine. Some might even say," Jane shifted and flicked her gaze away, "well, some might even say you're the stronger one out of the two of us. It takes a lot of guts to trust people, especially after you've been hurt. I build walls, and my skin is thick, hardly anything gets to me anymore. But the problem with thick skin is that everything becomes dull. Nothing can get through, not pain, of course, but nothing else either. Ultimately, thick skin makes you incapable of feeling the highs and lows of life. I think, before Ash taught me that, I would have eventually walled myself off so completely, I would have been like the walking dead."

She cleared her throat, shifting again. "So yeah, don't … just don't feel bad about being the way you are. I think you're great. And you know, we can't all be badasses like me."

I opened my mouth to respond, but words wouldn't come. I was shocked into silence. Ever since I'd come aboard The Pittsburgh, I'd been painfully aware of my perceived shortcomings. Zula was the genius, Masha the brilliant engineer, Jane the badass, and I was the healer. Sure, I wasn't useless, but I'd always considered myself the weakest link among the crew. The one who had to be protected from intense situations. I hated feeling that way and struggled to be more assertive, aggressive, and less fragile emotionally, but when it got down to it, I wouldn't be as talented a healer if I was less intuitive.

Jane stood, her lips curling up. "And yeah, Eron might not be my favorite person right now, but we'll get Zula and Masha back, so no harm no foul. Maybe he needs your brand of strength more than ever now." She turned to leave, pausing at my door. "Oh, and by the way, we have a prisoner. Thought you might want to join me for his questioning in a bit." The door slid open and she left without another word.

I sat up, my mind reeling. Jane was willing to put forgiveness on the table for Eron. Jane thought I was stronger than her. *I'm not. But maybe we're equally as strong in our own unique ways, just like she said.*

I swiped at the dried tear trails on my face, optimism buoying my mood. I'd been waffling back and forth with how to handle Eron … First claiming I would give him all of my trust, knowing I could heal him, before being stunned by the changes in him, and swinging back to fear and despair, and ultimately losing any hope of ever being with him again.

Maybe the answer lies somewhere in between.

I didn't have to be a badass like Jane to be a badass like me. I could stand in the path of adversity, unwavering in my beliefs. I would bend, but I wouldn't break, and I would heal Eron, even if it took the rest of my lifetime.

For I am Mazatimz, and that's what we do.

Without checking on Eron's current emotional state, I sent a surge of reassurance down the line to him, hoping it would take the edge off. For the moment, I didn't want to think about him anymore, my interest was piqued by the prisoner on the ship, and I wanted answers.

"Tamzy," Eron's voice whispered in my mind, startling me. It'd been years since he'd spoken to me that way, and it was disconcerting to have him pick now of all times to reach out to me in such a manner.

I thought about how badly I'd handled things from the beginning with our reunion. I pushed Eron too hard, expected too much from him too soon …

"Tamzy. I love you. None of it was your fault."

An image of his dull, lifeless eyes flashed in front of

me, causing bile to surge up my throat. That part he hadn't meant for me to get through our bond, it simply slipped in on the heels of his mental message before he could shut down the connection. Panic propelled me forward, and I dashed blindly from my room. *Eron, please don't do anything stupid.* I didn't know if he heard me, and I couldn't risk stopping to find out.

"Where are you going?" Jane demanded from behind me.

"Eron!" was all I managed. My heart thrashed against my ribcage, threatening to break free, and my limbs were numb, yet somehow they kept moving.

When I reached the prison, I skidded across the floor, my gaze riveted on the cell Eron was in. He was on the floor, but I couldn't tell much else since he'd closed off his side of the bond to me again. "Jane!" I screeched, hysteria riding me hard. "Jane, please!"

"What? What is it?" Jane entered the prison warily, not having a clue what was going on.

"Open it! Open it now!" The security grid went down, the lights fading as the door swung open. I rushed forward, dropping to my knees. "Eron!"

Blood. There's so much blood. A small blade lay on the floor in the growing pool of indigo. "No! No! Don't you dare die on me!" I searched frantically for the wound or wounds, Eron's shallow breathing and sluggish heart the only thing I could hear. "Why? Why can't I find it? I should be able to sense what's wrong."

Eron's eyes cracked open, his gaze unfocused. "It's for the best," he rasped. "You're safe now. I love you."

I knew in that instant why I couldn't find his wounds. Of course he would know I would rely on my healing abilities as a Mazatimz to search out the issue, which he was obviously interfering with. He'd also spread his blood around to be misleading. He was a half dozen steps ahead of me. I would have to do it the old-fashioned way.

Grimacing, I slid my hands along his body, starting with his wrists, and worked my way up his arms, watching his expression for a sign. I fully expected the wound to be somewhere unusual.

His lips curled up. "It's no use. I won't let you suffer anymore because of me. I realize now I'm too messed up in the head to know what's good for you and what's not. Now that I know you're safe here … It's better this way."

"No," I snapped. "And it's not too late, otherwise you wouldn't be conscious and able to put together coherent sentences. You're just being a dumb ass."

He chuckled, blood trickling out of the corner of his mouth. "I'm dying and you insult me."

"I insulted you because you're not going to die. I won't let you." I grinned, the blood coming from his mouth a clue. He'd injured himself in an obvious spot knowing I'd expect the opposite. "Nice try, though." I ripped his shirt up, revealing his stomach had been sliced open, the skin peeled back to show organs that should never be exposed to the light of day.

"How?" I sobbed, waving my hands around, gathering

energy. It was bad, but I could—*would* fix it. Or I'd die right along with him trying. It must have taken more determination than I could even begin to imagine to do such a thing to himself.

His eyes shut, his heartbeat slowing. "For you. I can do … anything … for you."

"Then you're going to live for me!" Shooting everything I had into him, I began to heal him from the inside out. Normally I would only use whatever energy I had to spare, but if I had to, I'd suck myself dry to save him. I'd do anything for him, too.

"No," he rumbled, "it's better if I die. I know I should never have contacted you … it ran the risk of you finding me too soon. But I wanted to tell you that I love you one last time. And none of it's your fault."

In defiance, I shot more healing energy into him, mesmerized as organs knit and disappeared behind fresh skin, a long, jagged scar forming in the shape of an S along his abdomen. *An S or a snake?* Was the shape of his wound another way to 'remind' himself of what he'd become?

I did one last scan of Eron's energies, collapsing across his chest when I was satisfied. He needed time to rest from the trauma, but he'd be fine in a matter of hours. The steady beat of his heart under my ear soothed me like nothing else could in that moment.

"Huh. So Mazatimz blood is purple. Guess I never thought about it," Jane muttered.

I uncurled myself from Eron, staggering to my feet. "Where did he get the blade from?"

Jane raised her hands, taking a few steps back. "I didn't search him like one of my bounties. I didn't think he'd … I never thought to … I'm sorry."

It wasn't her fault, and I knew it. I was merely looking for someone to blame, and she was the only one there and conscious. "I just can't believe he—I can't believe …" I crumpled into myself, flopping to the floor. The acrid scent of Eron's blood finally registered, causing me to gag. "I just got him back. I just … I can't—" Struggling to breathe, I flung myself over Eron again, clinging to him.

"Come on," Jane said, tugging on my arm. "Let's get this mess cleaned up, and then we can move him to where he won't be a danger to himself anymore."

I nodded numbly, my gaze sliding over Eron's prone form. Lurching down, I grabbed his cheeks, planting a hard kiss on his lips. The scent of blood and sweat lingered when I pulled away.

I wanted to say so many things to Jane, but the sentiments I longed to express were twisted up in my mangled insides. I was overwhelmed, which translated to an odd dulling of my mind and senses. "Mazatimz blood isn't really purple," I said, not sure where the words were coming from. "It just oxidizes differently than your blood."

Jane grunted and slid her arm around my shoulder for support. "Well, I hope I never have to see it again."

"Me too."

Chapter 16

Eron looked peaceful, his chest rising and falling in the easy pattern of a deep, healing sleep. I'd cleaned him off and dressed him in soft pants before strapping him down to a cot in the medical wing. I hated having to do it, but he'd proven himself a danger to himself.

Leaning in, I moved my hands through the air in a familiar dance, dipping in and around his energy fields, testing and assessing. Once satisfied, I sat down beside him, my gaze roaming his slack face. His eyes moved back and forth behind his lids. I wondered if he was dreaming about me … us? I hoped his mind was somewhere good, and not lost in the horrors he'd been forced to endure at Telvin. Tentatively I touched the scar on his stomach, tracing the length of it with my index finger.

How didn't I know how much he was suffering?

A lump formed in my throat, and my chest burned. He

seemed so small on the cot, younger, too, his brow smooth and worry-free. I thought it would be easy once we escaped Telvin. I thought if I just loved him enough everything would be fine. But the truth was, things might not ever be fine for Eron again. He'd been forced to go against his nature as a Mazatimz, and he could be broken beyond even my ability to repair. But that was okay because I would hold all of his pieces together. If he couldn't be strong then I would be strong enough for the both of us. Living without him wasn't an option. Not anymore. All of my uncertainty had been erased the instant I'd seen him covered in his own blood.

I pressed a soft kiss to his forehead, inhaling his scent. Sighing, I let my eyes slide shut, pretending for a moment things weren't so complicated. It was difficult for me, being a healer, to truly wrap my head around the atrocities other species seemed to revel in. *Why does there have to be so much suffering?*

A throat cleared behind me. "Ready?"

Straightening up, I turned to face Jane who was eyeing Eron. "I'd take Ash in any condition as long as he always comes back to me."

"No news from Ash yet?" I was honestly surprised. It wasn't like Ash to be absent when Jane needed him. Or maybe that was just it, maybe she didn't need him? Maybe she just wanted him. Since they'd bonded as phoenix mates, Jane possessed all of Ash's powers, even though she still struggled to control them most of the time. She was a lot harder to take down than she ever was before.

"No, nothing from Ash." She whirled around, leading the way to where our prisoner was being held by Dar.

"You seem calmer about it though?"

"That's because I have other things to focus on right now. Like getting the rest of my crew back."

"I'm sure Ash is fine."

We entered the engine room, and I glanced around in confusion, spotting Dar's large form looming over— "The creature!" I blurted.

"Good, you know him." Jane stalked forward, her hand twitching over the laser gun in her hip holster.

"Why are we doing this here? In the engine room? Now that Eron's no longer in the prison, why don't we—"

"Because I want to paint this room with his blood in tribute to Masha," Dar growled, his eyes dark with rage. I shuddered, getting a glimpse of why the rest of the Universe was terrified of Gartians. Mostly machine, it wasn't difficult to see how Dar's Gartian grade alloy enforced body could do major damage to anyone or anything he chose. I was glad he was on our side.

The threat seemed to be lost on the creature, though—as if Dar didn't even exist, he grinned at me. "Tamzea, so good to see you again. I've missed our time together."

A visceral memory washed over me, too powerful to ignore.

The creature's eyes twinkled with delight as he brandished a scalpel. Grabbing my wrist, he cut, my blood spurting out as he dug down to the bone. I was unable to move, to scream, having been injected with a drug to cause paralysis. But I could feel, and inside my head my screams ricocheted around my skull, the agony more than I'd ever had to bear.

Forcing myself to focus on the present, I blinked away the memory, involuntarily taking a step back, wanting as much distance between me and the creature as possible. I hated myself for demonstrating fear, wishing I could hide my emotions better.

The creature chuckled. "Ah, remembering some of the good times, I see. You were always one of my favorites to play with. I wish I'd had more time with you on your last visit. Unfortunately, other plans were in place for you."

"Go ahead, Dar," Jane growled, "make him sing."

A feral smile stretched across Dar's face. "My pleasure."

Metal met flesh and bone, rapid questions fired, and answers groaned. The air filled with the scent of blood and sweat, my senses tingling with awareness of someone nearby needing my brand of attention. I curled into myself, forcing my focus on the hum of the machinery surrounding us. Tension built within me, my need to help the creature—even though I hated him—rising within me. He suffered and therefore I needed to ease all I was able to.

"Stop!" I screeched, rushing forward. Without thinking I grabbed the creature's shoulders, my hands sliding over flesh slick with green-hued blood. My healing energy pulsed within me, and I pushed into the creature, sighing with relief as I eased the pain in both of us.

Dar wrenched me back, his expression wild. "What do you think you're doing?"

Not meeting his gaze, I hung my head. "I'm sorry. It's who I am."

"So pathetic," the creature croaked, disdain for me in his tone. "The Mazatimzs are a pathetic species. I enjoy your suffering, would relish in your death, and still you heal me without thought."

The moment stretched into what felt like an eternity, and finally, Jane spoke. "I shouldn't have brought her here. I thought maybe … well, I thought … never mind what I thought. I think he gave us all he is going to give. His prolonged torture is only going to make Tamzea suffer, too. You know what to do, Dar." She slid her arm around me, forcing me to move towards the door.

A thunderous snap echoed in my ears, followed by a sickening thud. My imagination conjured a half dozen unwanted images in that instant, all of which I pushed aside for my own sanity. The creature's lifeforce no longer registered on any level within me, so I knew the outcome of whatever had been done to him. I couldn't say I was sorry, and yet I was sad things like that had to happen. *The Universe truly is a depressing place.*

"So now what?" I rasped, leaning my head against Jane's shoulder.

"Now we go get Zula and Masha."

I nodded, my eyelids suddenly heavy. The latest nightmare we'd been subjected to because of the Denards couldn't end soon enough. Of course, unbeknownst to me, I'd been trapped in it for the last decade.

Chapter 17

Shifting nervously from foot to foot, I watched as Jane and Dar prepped their gear in the airlock. After much debate, aka a full-on shouting match, it was decided that I would stay on The Pittsburgh while Dar and Jane went to Telvin to retrieve Zula and Masha. It was still in question where Nina had disappeared to. The creature had claimed Telvin was only holding two of our crew members, but there was no other logical explanation of where she could have gone. Maybe they simply weren't acknowledging her as part of our crew since she herself was a Denard.

"Remember what I said to do if something happens to us," Jane instructed, her hands moving deftly over her various weapons. Old habits died hard since she didn't need laser guns and things of that ilk anymore with her fire powers. *Try telling her that though.*

I nibbled on my thumbnail. "The flight course is

already programmed into the computer. But I don't know why we don't get Gartian back up first."

"My people will only get involved if they must," Dar said. "And time is of the essence. We don't know what's being done to them."

"I don't like this. I have a bad feeling about all of it."

Jane rolled her eyes. "That's nothing new. You and Zula worry too much."

I snorted. "Really? It seems to me like we didn't worry enough this time."

Jane pulled her helmet on, her voice muffled. "Don't start up with that crap again. Telvin isn't the big baddie you make them out to be. I'll prove it by taking them down."

"*We* will take them down," Dar growled, his eyes flat, expression drawn in hard lines.

"All right. Just be careful."

Jane grinned. "Aren't I always?"

Sighing, I moved out of the airlock, shutting the door behind me. I peered through the small window, waiting for Jane's signal. She gave me a thumbs up, and I hit the button to equalize pressure and suck the air out. My stomach twisted when Dar and Jane propelled off the ship, attached to one another by a thin cord.

"Good luck," I murmured, before turning away.

Shuffling through the corridors, I made my way to the control room, where I could get a better view of Jane and Dar as they covertly made their way towards Telvin. It was still a bit disconcerting that the flight deck and control room had become one large space since the ship's overhaul. Before they had been stacked on top of each other, separated by a ladder, which I supposed was pointless and limiting. Obviously, the Gartians had thought so, too. One reason why Chimay grade ships weren't popular was because many thought they held design flaws. Of course, Jane thought the quirks were endearing, and had balked a bit at the prospect of changing anything.

Leaning closer to the window, I was able to track Jane and Dar easily since The Pittsburgh hovered dangerously close to the small space station, hidden under the Gartian cloaking device. My nerves pinged with anxiety. I'd never been on The Pittsburgh without Zula and Masha before. The small ship suddenly felt monstrous in size, threatening to swallow me up.

But I'm not alone. Not really. I have Eron.

I checked my wrist, where I'd synced my timepiece to alert me when five hours had passed. If I hadn't heard from Dar or Jane by then, I was to hightail it over to Gartian territory where I'd beg for help.

Resisting as long as I could, I reluctantly left the control room, making my way to the medical wing to see Eron. I could feel through our bond that he was still resting soundly, which meant there was nothing I could do for the time being but wait.

Wait. Wait. Wait. Wait for Jane and Dar. Wait for Eron to wake up. I'm tired of waiting. I need to do something.

"Tamzy," Eron whispered in my mind, hastening my pace.

When I reached the medical wing, Eron's eyes were open, staring straight ahead. "I didn't think you'd wake so soon." I made my way to his side, brushing a piece of hair from his forehead. *It's growing so fast now.* "How are you feeling?"

"Alive," he rumbled.

Leaning over into his field of vision, I narrowed my eyes, anger surging through my veins, scalding me. "Don't you ever do something so completely asinine again. Do you hear me? I can't believe—why would you—" Hot tears burst from my eyes, my chest tightening as I struggled to breathe.

Remorse wavered over Eron's features, his gaze unsure. "Tamzy, please, don't cry because of me. I don't think I can handle that right now."

I crumpled over his chest, pressing my face into hard muscle, winding my arms around him. I wanted to hold him even though he couldn't return the gesture since he was restrained. "Don't leave me. Don't you dare try to leave me again."

"I love you. I did it because I love you."

"That's a cop-out, a bunch of crap. You couldn't handle your plans being foiled and you panicked. What you did was the easy way out, and I don't care what you say otherwise."

"Nothing about leaving you could ever be easy."

Pulling away from him, I slapped him across the face,

internally cringing, and yet not regretting it at the same time. "You made the decision to take your life with such ease, which meant leaving me was easy. One minute you wanted to steal me away, and the next, when none of that worked out, you were attempting to end your life. Why? Why would you even consider such a thing? I don't understand any of it."

He worked his jaw back and forth, not bothering to heal the point of impact where a red palm print bloomed. "You wouldn't understand. You haven't been altered by Telvin as I have. I see things differently now. I can never be the male you need me to be. I thought … I thought I could. For an instant, I thought once we were away from here that I could be different for you. I allowed myself to hope—"

"You sold out my crew, Eron. You betrayed them and by extension me. And despite what I said, I would have forgiven you." I swallowed, glancing away from him. "You know I'd forgive you for anything."

"Let me out of these restraints." His voice was low and rough, caressing my insides.

I shook my head. "No. You can't be trusted."

"Please. I need to hold you."

I peered at him from under my lashes. "I can't. You managed to hide your intentions from me even with our bond. I have no idea who you are anymore. I want to trust, want to believe in you, but you've proven that I can't do either of those things."

His nostrils flared, and his jaw muscles flexed. "Maybe

you don't know pieces of me anymore, but you know the most important part: I love you. Nothing will ever change that."

"You were going to leave me!" My body shook uncontrollably, the truth of my words sinking in. Eron had tried to take his own life. It didn't matter how or why he'd attempted to leave me. When Telvin had ripped him from my life it'd been different, it hadn't been his choice. What he'd done in that cell when he'd torn into his own flesh … he'd decided to leave me behind, damn the consequences.

"I need to hold you. Now." His tone had taken on demand, no longer leaving room for my denial. I hated myself a bit for it, not being able to tell him no when I most likely should. One should only give another soul such power over them when it's been earned, and although Eron had deserved my devotion once, he'd lost the right when he'd betrayed me. And yet … yet …

I unbuckled his legs first, only hesitating for a moment before undoing his wrists. I whimpered when his strong arms encircled me, his chin resting on the top of my head. "I'm so confused, Eron. Nothing has made sense to me since Xia and Tia showed up. I'm all twisted inside. I don't know what to do about anything, and I can't decipher your motives, your actions are odd, out of character. I never thought—never considered the possibility that if you were still alive, that you'd be a stranger, and yet …" I leaned back enough to gaze up at his familiar face. "You're still my Eron. And I love you."

"I never thought I'd see you again, and I made peace with it, knowing that I'd sacrificed my life for yours. It didn't matter the monster I'd become because you'd never know." His fingers flexed against my back, his arms tightening around me. "And suddenly there you were again, the same girl I fell in love with, not altered by time at all."

Squeezing my eyes shut, I pressed my face back into his chest. "That's not true. I'm not the same. Besides mentioning the obvious, that I'm physically older, after I thought I'd lost you ... everything changed."

"But your soul hasn't changed. It takes someone truly astonishing to remain soft as you are amongst such cruelties. We've both been tested by our separation and only I failed."

"Soft?" My voice cracked. "You're calling me soft?"

"I don't have a better word for it, but it's meant as a compliment."

Ignoring him, I went on, "And I haven't been tested. Not here on The Pittsburgh. Not like you were."

"I missed you so much." His lips pressed against the top of my head.

"Then why would you try to leave me? It isn't love. Leaving someone behind to grieve you, that's not love."

He sighed heavily. "It seemed like the right thing to do at the time. I was lost. Some moments I remember what it was like to allow myself to hope, to be beckoned by your light, and others—others I fall into an abyss and I don't know which way is up or down. And when I'm there, in that vast darkness, the only thing I can think of is escape. I'm terrified that in the end, I'll drag you down, instead of you lifting me up."

I pounded a fist against the wide expanse of his back. "The next time you're lost, look to me for guidance. I can be strong enough for the both of us. You won't drag me down, I promise."

We fell into silence, our ragged breathing and erratic heartbeats filling my head. I wanted things to be fixed between us, but I knew we were far from where we needed to be.

"Eron, I—"

The Pittsburgh tilted abruptly, spilling us onto the floor in a tangle of limbs. The lights flashed to red, back to normal, and then red again, the alarm buzzing loudly in the background.

My heart plummeted into my feet. "We need to get to the control room. Now."

"Right behind you."

We raced through The Pittsburgh, panic riding me hard. *Are we under attack? But how?* No one knew we were there unless— *No.* Even if Jane and Dar had been captured, neither of them would give us up, especially after such a short period of time. It had to be something else.

I skidded into the control room, punching the buttons on the main computer with clumsy fingers. "Where the hell is it?" I snapped. No attack or breach was registering in any of the quadrants. "There. There it is." I tapped the screen, zooming in. "What? That can't be right."

But the computer wouldn't lie. We weren't under attack. No one knew where we were. We'd been hit by an asteroid, and although The Pittsburgh was reinforced by Gartian grade alloy, we'd been sent into a spin, something I wasn't equipped to handle. Nor was the autopilot, which had been sent into a tizzy from the impact, which was why the alarms had been going off.

"Eron. You wouldn't happen to know how to fly a Chimay grade ship, would you?"

He leaned over my shoulder, squinting at the data. "No. I have no idea."

"Didn't think so." I bit my lip, trying not to let panic overtake me. *What would Zula or Jane do?* Scurrying over to the flight chair, I strapped myself in. "Well, we're both about to learn, and hopefully we get good fast, otherwise we're going to be making an unscheduled crash landing on Telvin." I motioned to the chair next to mine. "Sit down, strap in, and get ready."

Eron visibly paled, but he followed my instructions.

Please let some of what I've seen Zula do over the past few years have registered. Please, please, please ...

Chapter 18

"What do I do?" Eron asked, his voice eerily calm.

I gave him a wan smile. "I don't know. You just being there helps, though."

Okay. Focus. Focus. Focus. I just have to steer. Simple enough. I glanced up at the navigation screen and squeaked. "Please tell me we're not upside down."

Eron leaned over and studied the screen, grimacing. "This ship has great gravity balance."

"What? What exactly does that mean?"

"You said not to tell you if we were upside down."

"What? I don't— Oh, forget it. Maybe I can loop up and around to right us."

Eron tapped the screen. "I think you should focus on not hitting Telvin first."

My eyes widened as I peered up at the screen again. "That wasn't there a minute ago!"

"It was there the whole time. You're the one who said we had to avoid crashing into it to begin with."

"Oh, well, shut up and help."

"I am helping. I just pointed out that you needed to worry about not crashing into Telvin before you worry about the ship being upside down."

I growled under my breath, "Zula always makes it look so easy."

Eron elbowed his way in next to me, taking over the controls. "Here. Let me."

I shoved back at him. "You said you didn't know how to fly a Chimay ship."

"That was before I saw how bad you were at it." He shot me a grin before rapidly punching buttons, all of which had begun to appear the same to me. *Maybe he has a point.*

I unbuckled my belt and shifted to the other seat, strapping myself in there. Telvin loomed in front of us, its shiny surface glinting in the light of a nearby star. "You need to pull more to the right! To the right! Eron—"

We lurched to the right, and I would have fallen out of my chair if not strapped in, but it wasn't enough. Telvin's image filled all the screens, The Pittsburgh on a collision course with it. I almost wanted to laugh. After everything we'd been through, a random asteroid was going to be our downfall.

Eron gritted his teeth. "Hold on, we're going down."

"You don't say?" Sarcasm dripped from my voice from bitterness at our situation.

Digging my nails into the arms of my chair, I braced myself for impact. Everything happened so fast. The ship's navigation system erupted in angry beeps, a warning that something large was in our path. *No shit.* A boom, a pop, and then metal scraping on metal filled the air before the lights flickered and all went still.

A few dozen heartbeats passed before I found the courage to move. On shaky limbs, I peeled myself from my seat, scrambling for Eron, who was staring straight ahead but not moving. Waving my hands through his energy field I checked him for any injuries.

"You're okay." I expelled one long breath.

Eron jerked to his feet, capturing my face with his hands. His gaze danced between my eyes just before his lips pressed hungrily to mine. Thoughts of it not being the time or place for affection flitted through my mind, quickly swept away with the spicy taste of Eron on my tongue, and the weight of his hard body pressing me into the computer console.

My hands glided down his back, settling on the muscular orbs of his ass. He groaned into my mouth, grinding against me. Breaking our kiss, he spun me around, yanking my pants down. He leaned over my back, plunging into me from behind. His fingers bit into the flesh on my hips, holding me steady as he slammed in and out of me. My head fell forward, the cold metal of the control panel soothing against my heated skin. I trembled, lost in all things Eron, surrounded by his energy, our bond open wide.

His name cascaded from my lips in reverie, turning into a moan as I spasmed around him. He erupted into me a moment later, collapsing along my back, his breathing erratic and in time with mine.

"That was ... sudden," I rasped, inhaling deeply.

Eron pulled away from me. "I wanted one last time with you, just in case."

My face flushed, and I stood, yanking my pants up. "Don't you dare start with that again."

"Shhh ... no." He cupped my cheek, staring into my eyes. "It's because of where we are."

"Telvin."

"Mmm hmm." His expression turned pensive. "They would have registered our impact, but if the cloaking system is still working I'm not sure if they could see us."

"But Jane won't know we're here either. What happens when her and Dar find Zula and Masha?" Jane hadn't taken one of The Pittsburgh's trackers, worried that Telvin would somehow get a hold of it. She'd been planning on relying on coordinates alone. Coordinates that were no longer relevant. "We have to go after them."

"No. We work on getting back into the air."

"Really? And who is going to help us with that? We barely landed in one piece, and now you think we're going to be able to fix anything that's wrong, let alone even know what, if anything, is wrong? We need Masha."

Eron's eyes danced with mirth. "I don't know. I think I did a pretty bang-up job flying this thing. I didn't blow us up or anything."

My mouth fell open. "Are you serious right now? What is wrong with you? We nearly died."

"But we didn't. Not even close. We'll figure this out. Don't worry."

Tilting my head, I studied Eron. His mood was lighter, his attitude practically jovial. And it all clicked into place. Each time we'd been intimate, for a short period afterwards, he was more like his old self, smiling, and even making jokes. It was the only time our bond was wide open. *I'm healing him through our bond ... through sex.* A giggle burst from my chest. "Oh, this is … this is …" I doubled over with laughter. Jane and Zula would never let me hear the end of it. *Which is why I'm never telling them.*

Thinking of Jane and Zula sobered me instantly. I couldn't simply stay on the ship when they were in danger. "We need weapons and space suits."

"You're serious about going into Telvin. Tamzy, no." He crossed his arms over his chest, scowling.

"I'm going, so you can either go with me, or you can stay here. The choice is yours." I pivoted on my heels and stalked from the control room.

"Tamzy, wait." Eron grabbed my arm, spinning me to face him. "I'll go alone. You stay—"

"No," I snapped. "I know I'll never be a badass like Jane, or a genius like Zula, or even a master mechanic like Masha, but I won't abandon my friends either." Jane had opened my eyes to the nature of my personal strength, which lay within my nature as a Mazatimz. I wasn't the obvious kind of strong, but when push came to shove, I wouldn't cower in the corner either. It didn't matter if I was terrified on the inside, just as long as I got the job done.

Eron nodded, acceptance changing his countenance. "All right, but I don't like it."

I snorted. "Yeah, I don't like it either, but it's what I need to do."

Chapter 19

Fidgeting, I ran my hand over the laser gun strapped to my hip. A fine tremor slithered up my spine, and I gritted my teeth, trying not to think about all the things it implied.

Eron and I were in the airlock, both of us clad in ill-fitting space suits and strapped with weapons that felt just plain wrong. I knew how to use a laser gun in theory, but this was different. I never thought I might actually be in a situation where I had to take someone's life. Even faced with the creature when he'd been suffering, I'd been helpless to stop myself from healing him.

"I'll do it if it comes to that."

I lifted my head to meet Eron's intense gaze. "What?"

He motioned to his own laser gun. "I've taken lives before. I'll do it again so you won't have to."

"No. I'll do what needs to be done."

He closed the scant distance between us, gripping my arms painfully. "And I'll make sure you don't need to."

I stared up at him, lost in the depth of pain peering out at me from behind his lavender eyes. I wanted to argue with him, protest his need to protect me, but I knew it would be pointless. Pulling away from him, I moved clumsily to the door. I lifted to my tiptoes, pressing my gloved hand to the glass. "Telvin isn't like any space station I've ever seen before."

"They didn't want anyone to mistake it for a supply space station. It would potentially invite unwanted questions. Most pass on by believing it to be some kind of moon, which is why it orbits that unsettled planet over there."

In the distance, I could see the tiny reddish dot, which was really a planet. "Why didn't they just build on the planet if it's unsettled?"

"Because they can move the space station if they need to."

I nodded. "Makes sense. And the way they built the outside of Telvin, with a surface like a moon … yeah, it all makes sense now. If I didn't know where we crashed I'd be confused about what we found."

"Exactly. Now let's get going … unless you've changed your mind?"

"No. We have to go after Jane and Dar. There's no other option."

Heaving a sigh, Eron pulled on his helmet without another word, and I followed suit, my heart quadrupling in time. *This is it. You can do this.* I slammed my hand onto the release, the outer door sliding open. I hesitated for only a moment before bounding off The Pittsburgh.

"Follow me," Eron's voice sounded through the tiny speaker in my helmet. He leapt in front of me, and I spun to make sure the cord attaching us didn't get tangled.

Even though I was with Eron, the space suits we were in gave me a sense of isolation, ratcheting up my nerves. The surface of Telvin was metallic, but duller than I'd expected, dents and scratches placed with clear forethought to make it less noticeable from space. The gravity was different, making the travel easier than it normally would be in our heavy gear. Although I didn't understand why Telvin didn't make the gravity more oppressive to accomplish the opposite.

"We'll get in through the maintenance hatch," Eron said, startling me from my inner musings.

"What if Jane and Dar were discovered and they know that's how they got in, too?"

"Then they won't be expecting more visitors, I hope."

I gulped. "Okay." So much could go wrong with our plan. In truth, we didn't have much of one. It consisted of three main points: get into Telvin, find Jane and Dar, and don't get caught.

Eron stopped short, and I leaned forward to get a better view when he crouched down to yank open a small hatch at his feet. He twisted around so I could see his face through the front of his helmet. "I'm going to have to unhook us. I'll go down the ladder first. I've never been in the maintenance tunnels myself, but I've seen the schematics. There aren't any lights, and it's going to be a tight fit. We'll have to get through on our hands and knees. Stay close behind me."

I gave him a thumbs up, accompanied by a brittle smile. *Okay. This is it. You can do this.* "I'm ready."

Eron unhooked the cord from his suit, and it hung in the air a second before his end dropped to the ground. I grabbed my end and wound it up, stuffing it into the small pocket in my space suit. And then he was gone, disappearing into the unknown. Sweat beaded on my upper lip, and I took a deep breath of the musty air in my suit. I forced myself to move, stretching my foot down into the opening, searching for the ladder. With each rung I descended, my breathing became a bit more erratic. I began to count —*in two, out two, in two, out two*—to keep myself from hyperventilating.

"You okay?"

I yelped, missing the last rung on the ladder, stumbling into Eron, and taking us both to the ground. "Don't do that," I snapped. "You startled me."

I could hear the mirth in Eron's voice when he spoke, "Don't talk? Sorry about that." He cleared his throat. "Okay, this is where we have to get down on our hands and knees to go through the tunnel. You ready?"

"Yes," I hissed. "Just go already."

"Switch on your helmet light. We won't have the light from above anymore once I go back up to close the hatch.

Leave your helmet on, too. I don't know where the airfields stabilize, it might not be until we're inside."

My cheeks flamed at the mention of the hatch. As the last one in, I should have remembered to close it, not that Eron was intentionally trying to make me feel guilty.

Eron's light popped on, and I blinked back spots as I reached up to turn mine on as well. He clambered up the ladder, sealing us in with the ominous thud of the hatch before returning. He then dropped to all fours, crawling into the small shaft to our right. I swallowed around the lump in my throat, gave myself one last internal pep talk, and lowered myself in after him.

My helmet light illuminated the back of Eron's suit and smooth metal walls. There was no dust or dirt, and no signs of unwanted critters either. I supposed Telvin didn't have the variance of visitors like supply space stations, which translated to pests that needed to be exterminated regularly. I shuddered at the thought of running into one of the nastier nuisances I'd witnessed scurrying about even on our ship before.

Eron stopped short, and I nearly ran into his backside. "What's wrong?" I hissed, my pulse leaping.

"Nothing. I just don't know which way to go."

"What do you mean you don't know which way to go? I thought you've seen the schematics?" *Not good. Not good. Not good.*

"I must have remembered wrong."

Remembered wrong? "Eron—"

"It's this way." He crawled to the right, and I followed.

Grinding my teeth together, I forced myself to stay silent. I wasn't going to start an argument with him, it wasn't the time or place, but I was fairly certain he was guessing which way to go. *Please let us be lucky and it's the right way.*

"We should be coming up to another ladder soon. When we get there, I'll go first and check—"

A loud clanging swallowed the rest of his words. "What was that?"

"Shit," he muttered. "Go back."

"Go back? Wha—"

"Just go back! Now!"

Since there wasn't enough room to turn around, I started crawling backwards, which wasn't as easy to do as it would seem. Blind panic caused me to slip and face-plant several times, but somehow we made it to the tunnel with the ladder.

"Eron? Tamzea?" Jane's voice echoed through the small space, and I whipped my head around to see her emerge from the same tunnel we'd just been in.

My mouth fell open, and I leaned against Eron in relief. "What are you doing down here?"

"We were coming to save you," Jane stated as if it was the most obvious thing ever.

Dar pulled himself from the tunnel, the fit much tighter than it had been for the rest of us. He grunted as he got to his feet. "I connected with the mainframe, and we saw the data about a ship crashing nearby. We figured it was you."

"And you were coming to save us," I finished for him.

Dar nodded.

I rolled my eyes. "We were coming to save you."

"You can't save us, we're saving you," Jane snapped.

"Obviously not."

"What about the rest of your crew?" Eron interjected.

Jane switched off her helmet light, glancing up the ladder impatiently. "They're being held on the other side of the space station," Jane muttered. "We thought it would be easier to enter somewhere else than traipse through the center of everything. At least from what information we gathered. We were going to help you and then get them. It wouldn't do us any good to rescue them when we wouldn't have a way off this place."

"We need Masha to get the ship back into space." I peered up at Dar, giving him an apologetic smile. "Sorry. I know you're good with that kind of stuff, but you're no Masha."

Dar shrugged, appearing not to care. "No one is as good as Masha."

Jane sighed heavily. "Okay, so you two go back to The Pittsburgh, and Dar and I will head back in." She nodded in the direction of the tunnel. "It'll be more difficult making our way through the hub of things, but it's doable. Right, Dar?"

"I will paint the walls with the blood of any being who stands in my way of getting to Masha."

"I'll take that as a yes." Jane patted Dar's arm. "You need

to tone down the intensity just a bit, okay? At least until it's needed."

Dar didn't respond, and instead turned and dropped down on all fours, heading back into the tunnel.

I caught Jane's gaze, narrowing mine. "We're not going back. You might need us." She opened her mouth to speak and I cut her off. "Don't you dare order me as my captain. Don't you dare! We're here. We've come this far, and we're helping."

Jane studied me for a moment before reluctantly nodding. "Fine. Don't make me regret it though." She dropped down and crawled into the tunnel.

Eron grabbed my arm. "You sure about this?"

"You don't have to come if you don't want to." I wasn't sure why I said it. I knew Eron would go wherever I went.

He snorted. "I can tell you know I won't leave you. Your emotions don't lie even when your lips do."

"Whatever," I mumbled, heading into the tunnel after Jane.

Discovering that Jane and Dar hadn't been captured had gone a long way in relieving some of my anxiety. Now there were four of us, and we just had to focus on getting to Zula and Masha. Our odds of success had doubled … at least that's the way I saw it.

The four of us crawled slowly through the tunnels, the walls seemingly closing in on us. I concentrated on regulating my breathing to keep myself from panicking completely. When we finally made it to a second ladder, I wanted to jump for joy.

"Up we go," Jane muttered, her voice breaking the silence.

The ladder led to a small room, which was piled high with supplies and boxes. I yanked off my helmet and gloves, wiping sweat from my face with the back of my hand.

"Now what?"

"Me and Dar are going after Zula and Masha. I want you two to monitor our progress and let us know if the shit's about to hit the fan. We'll show you where Dar hacked into the mainframe. Got it?"

I couldn't help the smile that spread across my face. Eron and I would be helping, and yet we wouldn't be in the thick of things. It was the ideal situation for me. "Yep, we can handle that."

Dar led the way over to the corner of the room, moving several boxes to reveal a panel with exposed wires. Pulling a small device from a pack on his hip, he attached it to several other pieces he had stored in a hollow compartment in his metal arm. He made quick work of building what appeared to be a small computer, complete with video feed.

Dar straightened himself, seeming pleased with his work. "This is hooked into the mainframe. You can access the surveillance cameras and any other information you might find pertinent in aiding us." He stalked away, fresh determination on his face.

Jane tapped the communicator on the inside part of her suit. "We'll be in touch." She dropped her helmet on the floor next to the rest of ours before dashing after Dar.

Settling cross-legged on the floor, I glanced up at Eron. "See, this doesn't seem so bad, does it?"

He scowled. "I don't like it. It's all too easy."

I focused in on the small screen, squinting at the black and white images that flickered every couple of seconds, switching between different camera views. "Maybe taking the creature out has them a bit off-kilter."

"He was just one of many. There are a dozen more identical to him. His demise won't mean anything."

I shuddered, an image of an army of creatures skittering across my brain. "Then why was he the only one I ever saw?"

"It wasn't the same creature. He is from a race who are legion, for lack of a better term, and they share memories, their thoughts, and emotions."

"I've never heard of a species like that before. Huh." I shifted, suddenly uncomfortable. As much as I hated to admit it, I'd been relieved when Dar ended the creature's existence. But he'd only killed one of many, which explained why no one from Telvin had sent a retrieval party of any kind for the creature. I'd thought they simply didn't care, and I was right on one level. "So all of them, the entire species, are exactly like—"

"Yes. They're all like him."

"Females?"

"They don't need them."

I focused in on Jane and Dar on the screen, so far they

hadn't run into anyone from Telvin. It seemed … odd. Something wasn't right. "We need to access as much information while we're here as we can—files, data, whatever we can get our hands on. I want to know what Telvin's master plan is." The experiments, the abductions, not just of Mazatimzs, but of other species of all walks of life. There had to be a method to the seeming madness, and I wanted to know what it was.

"Here, let me. I at least have a better idea of what to look for." Eron crouched beside me, his fingers flying over the controls. Text and diagrams, photos and schematics, appeared and disappeared on the screen. I had a hard time reading anything with how fast Eron was flipping through everything.

"This." He slapped his open palm against the tiny screen. "This is what we're looking for." He leaned in, eyes narrowed as he scanned the hand-written words.

"What is it? Why is it hand-written?"

"It's from a journal. I've been searching for this ..." His eyes darted back and forth, his face paling.

"You need to check back in on Jane and Dar."

"I will, I just need— Shit. It's incomplete. We need to find the actual journal. I know it's here in the facilities somewhere. I got a glimpse of it once."

I drummed my fingers along the floor. "Please check back in on Jane and Dar." I couldn't help feeling like something bad would happen if we didn't have our eyes on them. I'd been the one wanting to check for other information, but I figured we could flip back and forth.

"I will, just let me—"

"Now!" I snapped, leaning over Eron to do it myself.

Eron growled in frustration, and I sighed in relief as an image of Jane and Dar moving through the Telvin corridors unharassed appeared on the screen. "Okay, you can go back to the journal now."

"Thanks." Eron's annoyance washed over me through our bond. He stiffened, his head whipping in the direction of the door. "Did you hear that?"

I dropped my voice to a whisper, tension tightening all my muscles. "No. What is—"

"Hide. Someone's coming."

It was then I heard the door unlock, creaking open slowly. We scrambled to cover Dar's equipment and to hide ourselves behind the stacks of supplies nearby. I squeezed my eyes shut, keeping my breathing shallow as I tried to remain perfectly still. Eron's hand slid over mine, his energy humming through me.

It'll be fine. They don't know we're here. Whoever is in here has no reason to look for us.

It'll be fine. Fine ... fine ... fine.

Chapter 20

An eternity passed while we were in that corner. My heart threatened to explode in my chest, dizziness assaulting me. If not for Eron, I was sure I would have had a complete meltdown. As it was, I was a millisecond away from passing out.

I could hear things being shifted around as if someone was searching for something specific. *Find it. Find it now and get out before you find us instead.*

Eron leaned into me, his lips skimming my earlobe. My eyes popped open with alarm. *What are you doing?* I demanded using ocular communication only. His lavender gaze glinted with mischief and something else I couldn't quite read with my growing panic. In response to my question, he captured my lips with his, swirling his tongue against mine. I wasn't sure I was capable of reciprocating any kind of affection, although I did get lost in the feel of Eron's hard body pressing into me. My nostrils flared, my chest fully expanding with air, a sense of relief washing over me to quickly be replaced with a jolt of lust.

Eron pulled away from me abruptly, a grin spreading across his face. "They're gone."

I blinked a few times. "What?" *He did not just do what I think he did.* "You kissed me as a distraction." I wasn't sure how to feel about that.

His grin widened. "Yeah. It worked, didn't it? You were about to have a first-class freak-out. I had to do something, and it was the only thing to pop into my mind."

I grunted, awkwardly pulling myself to my feet. "Jane's right. Males of all species are run by one thing."

"It wasn't like I was planning on having sex with you right here."

"Mmm hmm … we don't have time for this. We need to check in on Jane and Dar. We need—"

"To find that journal," he interrupted.

"Why is it so important?"

"It's old. Very old. And it has answers we won't find anywhere else, at least assessable answers."

Well, at least the old part explained why it was handwritten, and if it was incredibly important, like Eron claimed, then it would make sense why it would have been preserved in multiple ways. "Where is it?"

"I may be able to track it through the database. I've never had complete access until now." Eron was already typing away before I could respond. It was clear it didn't matter what I would have said on the matter, though. He considered the journal more important than checking in on Dar and Jane like we were supposed to be doing.

"Just check back in on Jane and Dar again before you continue your search, please."

As if I hadn't spoken, Eron continued searching. "Found it!" He jumped to his feet, his excitement tangible. "It's locked in the secondary archives. Now that I know where it is, it shouldn't be difficult to steal."

I quirked an eyebrow. "And just where are these secondary archives?"

"It'll be fine." Eron hurried to the door.

"Umm … that didn't answer my question. And where do you think you're going?"

"Stay here and monitor everything. I'm going to get the journal."

Grabbing his arm, I was dragged a few feet across the floor. "You're not going without me. I'm not sitting here waiting for everyone. I-I can't let you go without me." The truth was, I didn't have an issue with staying behind if it wasn't Eron doing the leaving. After being separated from him for so long, I had a sudden and irrational fear that if I let him walk out that door without me, I'd never see him again.

He tilted his head, understanding dawning in his eyes. "All right. Follow me."

As we made our way through Telvin, I couldn't help but be reminded again of how all over the place Eron's emotions and actions were. I had no idea how he was going to be from one moment to the next. It was giving me emotional whiplash, to say the least.

"No. I'll retrieve it before the next procedure," a male voice said from behind us.

Eron yanked me into a nearby room, covering my mouth with his hand. "No one saw us. Stay calm." His hot breath fanned across my cheek, and I nodded.

Heavy footsteps moved past us, slow and steady, not giving any signs of stopping. I exhaled with relief through my nostrils. Eron and I waited another few moments before heading back out into the hallway.

Swiping at sweat from my brow, I struggled to keep pace with Eron. His legs were longer, and he didn't seem to be as affected as I was by the heat of our space suits. They were meant to insulate against the cold of space, not be worn to jog around in.

Sensing my distress, he murmured, "Not too much farther, I promise."

Biting my lower lip, I wondered what would happen if we weren't there when Jane and Dar got back with Masha and Zula. I hadn't even considered it until that moment. *Crap.* "Hurry," I snapped. "We need to get back before everyone else does."

"They have to make it to the other side of Telvin and back. Trust me, we'll be where we need to be before they get there."

However, being back in time wasn't my only concern. With all the cameras in Telvin set up for surveillance, I couldn't help but wonder why no one seemed worried about any of us being spotted. Maybe they were only viewed after the fact, or if a breach in Telvin was already suspected. I decided to keep my mouth shut about my concerns, it wasn't the time or place to pepper Eron with more questions. It would only slow us down.

Coming to metal double doors, Eron paused to punch in a security code, swearing when nothing happened. "I should have figured they changed the codes since I left, but I was hoping they didn't get a chance yet."

I ground my teeth together, fighting the urge to snap at Eron for being so cavalier about the whole situation. Instead, I plastered a fake smile on my face, shrugged, and said, "Oh well, we tried. We better head back."

Eron unholstered his laser gun, firing at point black range at the door panel. Wires fizzled and frayed, the scent of burnt metal and plastic singeing my nostrils. The door slid open a moment later. He smirked, before swaggering into the room.

"You could have just as easily fried the circuits so the door wouldn't open. You had a fifty-fifty chance." I'd been around Jane long enough to see how that worked firsthand. Eron wasn't the only one who liked to get a bit trigger-happy.

"It all worked out though." Eron headed for a safe in the wall, another security panel next to it.

"Is it me?" I wondered out loud, scuffling along behind Eron. "Do I bring out the reckless behavior in everyone?"

"Stand back." Eron fired his laser gun again, laughing

when the safe swung open a moment later. "I think I'm starting to see the merit in having one of these things."

"They aren't meant to open locks, Eron." Crossing my arms over my chest, I leaned against the wall, the heat from my suit staggering.

"Let's go." Eron hurried towards the door, glancing over his shoulder at me. "What are you waiting for?"

I scowled, pushing off the wall and forcing myself into motion even though I was pretty sure my skin was melting off. "Did you at least get the stupid journal?"

"Well, well, well, what do we have here?" a familiar male voice asked. "Didn't expect to see either of you again."

I froze, the shock of the creature being alive and well after what happened on The Pittsburgh jarring. *It's not the same creature. They're legion.*

Fumbling for my laser gun, I backed up a few steps. "Get out of our way." Thankfully my voice didn't tremble like my insides. "I'm a surprisingly good shot." I lifted the gun, sighting the creature's malicious sneer.

"You don't have it in you. You're not a killer … like Eron," the creature sneered, stalking forward.

"That's right. She's not." Eron squeezed off several shots, hitting the creature in his chest, dropping him to the ground. The acrid odor of burning flesh filled the air, and I gagged back bile.

I crept forward, my gaze riveted on the prone form of the creature. His dull, lifeless eyes stared up at nothing. *Eron did that. Eron killed him.* I knew he'd killed, and tortured, been forced to do horrible things by Telvin—I'd seen some of those things in my nightmares—but experiencing him commit murder firsthand was something else entirely. My heart beat erratically as I struggled to get my mind around it.

He pulled the trigger. He ended another's life. Just like that. Of course, there was no denying that the creature was a threat to us. He would have certainly done worse to Eron and me if he'd been given the opportunity. The creature tortured for fun. He enjoyed his job at Telvin, it wasn't hard to sense.

What makes certain beings so cruel and others kind? Why are some capable of committing such atrocities and others unable to do the simplest things to even protect themselves? And what does it say about Eron that he can be both? Cruel and kind, gentle and—

"Tamzy!" Eron took me by the shoulder, peering down at me as he shook. "We don't have time for this right now. Snap out of it."

Blinking, I registered that at some point I'd fallen to my knees. "I-I'm sorry."

Eron smoothed a few pieces of hair that had escaped my braids out of my face. "It's okay. I understand. But are you okay now?"

"Yeah, I'm okay now." I let Eron help me to my feet, his arm sliding around my waist.

He pressed his lips to my temple, murmuring against my skin, "I love that none of what you've suffered has changed you. I'll do the dirty work for you, just like I promised. I won't let this place, or any other, taint you. I won't let the Universe take something as beautiful as your compassion and turn it cold."

It was easy to read between the lines of what he was saying. He didn't want me to be tainted … like he was. He didn't want the Universe to steal my compassion … as it had from him. He wanted to protect me from becoming like him, which saddened me. He saw himself as broken, and although he was on so many levels, I refused to accept his self-loathing. What had been done to him was out of his control, which meant he shouldn't blame himself.

"Stop it," I hissed. "It's not the time or place for this conversation, but we are going to have it." Standing on my tiptoes, I threaded my hands into his hair, yanking his face down to mine. "And until we hash out this ridiculousness that you keep on spewing, I don't want to hear one more word about how you're—"

Agony twisted my gut, fast and sharp, like someone had stabbed me, and I fell away from Eron, reeling as I attempted to figure out what was wrong. *It's not me. It's—*" Torture," I gasped out. "Someone is being tortured nearby."

Eron narrowed his eyes in concentration. "I feel it, too."

I leaned into him for support, staggering as he led us out of the room and into the hallway. "Hang on, Tamzy. Just hang on."

Black spots danced in front of my eyes, my world tilting sideways. I didn't understand why I was being affected in such a way. It wasn't unusual for me to feel others' pain, but not in the literal sense, although it wasn't unheard of for Mazatimzs to experience such things. It had to be because I wasn't used to the power boost with Eron so near to me. He had blocks. I didn't.

Eron leaned me against a wall, and I slid down to the floor, curling in on myself. "Tamzy, I— Shit. I'll take care of this."

A door slid open, an ear-piercing scream meeting my ears. I clutched at my middle, wanting … needing to make it stop. *Pain. Too much pain.* Clawing at the floor, I somehow managed to get to my feet, and I lurched into the room, completely unaware of everything except the child strapped on a table.

My eyes widened, time standing still, as I took in the scene before me. Eron brandished his laser gun, squaring off with the creature, again. Several more of the creatures rushed forward, intent on stopping Eron from taking another of them down. On the table was a humanoid child, species unknown. It was difficult to tell with blood covering its face and body. It writhed in pain, oblivious to what was going on around it. But that wasn't the worst of it. Along the wall, in cages barely large enough to contain even their small bodies, were dozens more humanoid children, all of their expressions filled with terror.

Children. They're all just children. Fury like I'd never experienced morphed into blind rage, and I whirled around, my arms stretching out on instinct. *Unacceptable. This is … wrong. Completely unacceptable. I. Will. Make. Them.*

All. Pay. Without another thought, I yanked on all of the creatures' lifeforces, somehow penetrating their energy when I'd never been able to before, and drawing all of it to me. *None of you deserve to live. They're just innocent children.*

The creature, each one of him, dropped like boulders, instantly dead. But I didn't stop there. I reached out with my senses beyond the room we were in, searching for all of them. Every single one. *None of you deserve to live.* I could feel every living being in Telvin, and every single version of the creature.

I killed them all without moving from that tiny room.

When I'd finished, dizziness assaulted me, my heart pounding against my eardrums. I swayed, Eron catching me in his arms before I could hit the ground. I smiled, gazing up into his beautiful eyes. "They'll be safe now. The children. They're all safe. I saved them."

I fell into darkness.

Chapter 21

I came to instantly, fully aware of what forced me into temporary oblivion. Groaning, I rubbed my temples, Eron's face filling up my vision. Sadness radiated from him, stifling all of my own emotions.

"I didn't want that for you." He brushed a thumb across my cheek. "I never wanted any of it for you. I was supposed to be your shield. It was the one thing I had left to give me purpose."

I grabbed at his hand, but he flinched away from my touch. "Don't. I may not have planned to ever kill anyone, but it was necessary. They're children. You can't be my shield, not like you want. Being that for me was not your only reason to go on. I love y—"

Eron stood, essentially ending our conversation. He offered me his hand, and I slid mine into his, letting him help me up. I glanced around the room, grimacing. "We need to get them out of here." I nibbled my bottom lip, considering our options. "And not just the children in this room. I felt the lifeforces of too many to count. Different species and different ages, all being held by Telvin. Or they were." I hadn't felt any other presences associated with the Telvin side of things besides the legion known as the creature. Where had everyone else gone?

"We have full run of the place now. Which makes me suspicious. We need to evacuate everyone we can as soon as possible."

"I agree," I said, moving towards the child strapped to the table. I could tell Eron had already healed it the best he could, the wide black eyes no longer filled with physical pain. "It's going to be okay," I mumbled, giving the child a warm smile. I reached down to unbuckle it, still unsure of its gender and species. It was humanoid, but bald, its eyes completely black. I couldn't tell much else with so much dried blood covering it. "I'm just going to—"

It screamed, the sound terror-ridden. I shrank back, glancing at Eron. "Why is it afraid of me?"

Eron tapped behind his right ear. "It doesn't know what you're saying." He motioned to the cages. "None of them do. And most of them probably recognize me."

Oh, right. I should have realized that. And of course, none of them would have translator implants. I fanned myself, the heat from my suit getting to me again. I wasn't quite sure how to handle frightened children who couldn't understand a word I was saying. "So what do we—"

"There you are!" Jane burst into the room, Dar and Masha hot on her heels.

"Masha!" I exclaimed, rushing over to crush her in a hug. "I'm so relieved you're okay." I stepped back, moving my hands through her energy field, just to make sure. I nodded to myself. "Mmm hmm ... you're fine. And what about—" It was then I registered the lack of Zula's presence.

Jane frowned. "She's not here, and we couldn't find a sign of her anywhere. We're going to have to check the surveillance records to see where they took her, or if she was even brought here to begin with."

"Dar, help me!" Masha was frantically trying to free the child on the table, her hands fumbling with the buckles. The child was mumbling something to Masha, relief etched into its tiny features.

I gasped. "They're all Guavivas." They weren't children at all. Guavivas were born with a glamour to protect them, making them appear to be child-like even after they'd reached adulthood. It was a survival mechanism for their species, and not many knew about it. I could see past the glamour when I was looking for it, but I'd somehow missed it under the stress of the situation.

"Yes, it's why they're kept in this room, away from machines," Eron said.

It was only then I noticed the room was lacking all signs of modern technology. It was to keep the Guavivas from using machines to help them escape. Obviously, Telvin had known what they were dealing with when it came to their species. *How do they know so much about so many?* The Guavivas guarded their secrets well, and the only reason I knew as much as I did was that Masha trusted me, and I needed to know in order to work with her energy fields. Until recently, Jane hadn't even been privy to the information about Masha using glamour to hide her true appearance.

"Masha, you and Dar take care of everyone here," Jane commanded, "we're going to free the rest of the prisoners, and check the surveillance for Zula."

"Eron and I will take care of freeing the other prisoners. We'll be able to sense where there are energy fields and we can heal anyone who needs it. You find Zula."

Jane clapped her hands together. "All right, yeah. Sounds like a plan. Now go!"

I grabbed Eron's hand, tugging him after me. "Come on! We need to hurry!"

I couldn't shake the feeling that everything was too easy, just like both times I'd escaped from Telvin before, and I'd been right. The fact that only the creature, or creatures, had been left on the space station worried me. Were we all being set up yet again? Probably, but what other choice did we have at the moment? None, as far as I could tell.

"Here." I skidded to a stop in front of a white door, one of many that were essentially identical.

Eron shot the keypad, giving me a sidelong glance before entering the room ahead of me. Inside was a large male, class unknown. His skin was covered in black and white fur, his features a cross between a human and a long-extinct Earth tiger. Recognition washed over me, and I struggled to remember what I knew about him, besides the fact that he'd been our bounty on The Pittsburgh before I'd been taken by Xia and Tia. I just assumed he'd been dropped off, but apparently, I'd been wrong. *Shit. What was he wanted for? Is he dangerous?*

"Who are you?" he growled, his voice gravelly. "Not that I'll be able to understand you." He flashed sharp teeth, but there was no recognition for me as far as I could tell, which boded well for our chances. I usually didn't interact in any way with the bounties Jane brought in, and this one probably didn't notice me when Jane dragged him, kicking and screaming, to our ship's prison.

Pushing in front of Eron, I motioned to my hair and eyes, hoping the man-tiger would know what it meant. If he didn't know who I was in relation to Jane, then the Mazatimz good name shouldn't be tarnished in his eyes.

The man-tiger nodded. "Mazatimz, yes, I know what you are. And in space suits. Please tell me that means I'm getting out of here."

Grinning, I nodded enthusiastically, waving with a flourish for him to follow us. The man-tiger loped along behind us with no hesitation.

"I haven't seen his kind before," I said to Eron. "Do you know what he is?" Even Zula hadn't known when he'd been brought in. We only knew what his profile in the system had shared, which was Class 4, species unknown.

"No idea. Maybe a hybrid of some sort. More species are springing up every day in the far corners of the galaxies."

It was true. Cross-species mating wasn't common, but not unheard of. It wasn't that different species were opposed to the idea in theory, but a lot came down to simple attraction. Even if I didn't have Eron, I could never imagine getting down and dirty with the man-tiger, for instance. He was more beast than man for my taste.

I focused on sensing lifeforces, leading our trio to another door a few down from where we'd found our first rescue. Eron and I entered, motioning for the man-tiger to stay. He came along with us anyways.

Damn, I'm really beginning to appreciate the translator implants. Not having them is making this more difficult than it needs to be.

And so it went, Eron and I rounded up the prisoners of Telvin, most of them in decent shape. Those who were too weak to walk were carried by others, even though most were unable to understand each other's languages. Only a few species were found in duplicate, but all caught on pretty quickly that we were on a rescue mission. There were about forty prisoners with us when we finally returned to where we'd left Masha and Dar.

Masha was sitting cross-legged on the floor, murmuring reassuring words to the group of Guavivas clustered around her. Dar hovered nearby, watching like a silent sentinel.

My brow furrowed with worry as I glanced around the rest of the room. "Jane's not back yet?"

"No," Dar rumbled.

My finger hovered over the communication link in my suit, but I was afraid I'd interrupt her at a precarious moment. Instead, I sent my energy outward, searching for her lifeforce. "I'm not getting anything." When I thought about it, we should have run into her at some point, since I'd been generically searching for any lifeforce. "Can you sense her?" I asked Eron, whose lips were pressed into a thin line.

"No. I can't do some of that anymore."

Surprise rocked through me, and I wondered if he physically was incapable or if it was a mental block. However, I'd have to find out later. For the time being, finding Jane, and hopefully information on Zula, was my top priority. "Okay. Well, we need to track her down. I'm not comfortable being here longer than we have to be."

"I'm here," Jane grunted. I wasn't sure why I hadn't been able to sense her, but I was guessing fatigue was the likely answer. She limped into the now very crowded room, dragging behind her a metal cart, Xia on the top part, and Tia on the bottom, both of them unconscious and tied up.

Eron stepped in front of me, his voice harsh. "Why did you bring them here? You need to kill them before they can do any more damage." He reached for his laser gun, his intentions clear.

"No! Stop!" I lunged in front of him, batting the gun from his hand. "You can't kill them."

Eron glowered, his gaze flicking away as he dipped down to retrieve the gun, sheathing it in its holster. "Telvin used our DNA to build them, but no matter what you think they're not our children. They'll kill you if given the chance."

"But not you?"

"No. At least not before. But who knows how long it'll take before that changes."

"We don't have time for this discussion," Jane interrupted. "I'm bringing them with us, and we can decide what to do with them once Telvin is a few light slides away."

"We have a bit of a communication problem," tiger-man growled, his furry face scrunched up in confusion as a scaled, red female waved her arms in front of him in frustration. He glanced up, his gaze darkening when it landed on Jane. "You."

Jane stared blankly at tiger-man, tilting her head. "Do I know you?"

When she didn't move, tiger-man glanced at Eron. "She doesn't recognize me?" Eron shook his head and shrugged, his body language clear. "Well, then I guess we don't have a problem."

"A problem with what?" Jane demanded, narrowing her eyes.

Moving in front of Jane, I glared up at her. "Forget about it. We don't have time for trivial things. Plus, he can't understand you, remember? This is a one-sided conversation at the moment."

Jane grunted, her attention already moving on, and I heaved a sigh of relief, doing the same.

Not needing the few of us with translators to attempt to bridge the communication gap would make things easier after we got everyone on The Pittsburgh. Unfortunately, I didn't have enough to cover all of the new passengers. "Right. Eron, do you know if there are any translator implants stored anywhere in Telvin?"

"Maybe. I'm not sure what was done with the ones they removed from everyone once they're brought here."

I fanned myself, sweat dribbling from every pore. "If they're in working order, sanitizing them won't be a problem. Any ideas where they might be if they weren't tossed out?"

Anger burned within me when I thought about how every single person in that room, Dar and Jane aside, had been treated when they'd been taken by Telvin. All of our basic rights had been swept right out into space like we were nothing more than objects instead of living, breathing, sentient beings. Science had a history of being cavalier with lives, and many medical advancements in numerous fields had been made thanks to such attitudes. But to me, a Mazatimz, such tactics were beyond my comprehension.

Eron squeezed my shoulder, forcing me to focus on him. "Calm down. You need to focus on the task at hand before you let the rage take over."

"I don't have—"

"You do. And it's my fault you feel it now. For that, I'm sorry, too." He turned, walking slowly from the room, his shoulders slumped.

I glanced at Jane. "You get what we need to find Zula?"

"Hope so. But don't worry, I'll find our Smurfette if it's the last thing I do."

Satisfied, I darted after Eron, grabbing his arm. "Where do you think you're going?" There couldn't be a worse time for one of his emotional breakdowns. He needed to keep it together until we got back to the ship, where I could take care of him.

"I was going to check for extra translator—"

Telvin shook, the lights flickering. "No time." I spun around, Jane dashing out of the room, Dar, Masha, and the ex-prisoners crowding behind her. We all could guess what we'd been dreading was about to happen. Everything had been too easy so far.

"We need to get out the same way we came. Our helmets ..." She glanced over her shoulder, swearing under her breath. "We're going to have to get to the ship and come back for the rest of them. I don't know what the air is like out there on the surface."

"Should be fine," Masha spoke up. "I was wondering why all of you were in space suits. Didn't you notice that there weren't any airlocks or seals when you came in?"

I realized Dar had shucked his space suit, obviously coming to that conclusion on his own. "Great. I've been wearing this oven for absolutely no reason." Apparently, there was no type of air bubble or shield set up within Telvin, it was around Telvin. It was advanced technology, the kind we didn't even have on The Pittsburgh, but we hadn't figured Telvin wanted to encourage exploration by anyone who crashed on the pretend moon. I tugged at the zipper on my suit, but Jane grabbed my wrist.

"Hey, you need to bring that with us. Those things are expensive."

I grimaced. "I'll move faster without it."

Telvin shook again, the main lights going out completely, submerging us in the dark for a few heartbeats, before the backups came on.

"Follow me!" Jane waved her hand. "Bring them," she commanded to Dar, pointing at Xia and Tia.

Jane led the way, Eron and I close behind her, Dar pushing the cart with Xia and Tia on it, followed by everyone else. No one spoke, so much as grumbled under their breath. Fear of what was happening kept all of us focused on getting the hell out of Telvin.

I knew it wasn't going to be easy in the end.

Chapter 22

I wasn't claustrophobic, but with Telvin threatening to fall down around our ears, and me crawling on all fours through a narrow tunnel, people in front and behind me … yeah, I was dangerously close to having a meltdown.

"Not too much farther," Eron's voice in my helmet caused me to jump. I'd been forced to put the stupid thing back on because I couldn't crawl and carry it at the same time. Jane was confident enough of our escape that she wouldn't let me sacrifice a perfectly good space suit. One that I hadn't needed to begin with, apparently.

My erratic breathing was almost deafening in my helmet, causing me to feel isolated. If not for the steady hum of Eron's presence through our bond, I would have thought myself completely alone, despite having people all around me. My senses were off, nerves keeping me from using my abilities.

Eron pulled himself to his feet, reaching back to help me onto the ladder. Once we got going his head swiveled back every few seconds to check on me.

"Up! Up! Up! Faster! Faster! Faster!" Jane called from above, her voice strained, which ratcheted up my pulse. If she was nervous then we all had reason to fear.

"Calm down. We're almost there," Eron said, his tone calm—too calm.

I had no choice but to press forward, and hope for the best. "How are we going to get Xia and Tia up here?" I wasn't even sure how Dar had planned on getting them through the tunnel. Pushing them maybe? I hadn't put much thought into the logistics.

"We should leave them behind," Eron stated with the same calm tone to his voice. "Those two are abominations."

My foot slipped on one of the rungs, the front of my helmet hitting my hands. Thankfully it didn't hurt enough to force my fingers to let go automatically. Finding my balance again, I glared at the back of Eron. "It's what they were taught. It can be untaught. They're just children."

"They're pure evil. They enjoy the things they do. You have no idea."

"It can be untaught," I grated.

"And who's going to teach them the right ways? You? Me? You know they won't be accepted by our people."

It was true. We couldn't send them to our people for rehabilitation. If things didn't work out, the Mazatimzs would banish them, which wasn't much better than a death sentence. "I'll figure it out. We can't let them die."

"*You* can't let them die. I'd be fine with it."

I bit my lower lip, tasting blood. Did he mean that, or was he saying it because he wanted to believe it? Even with our bond, I couldn't tell.

When I reached the top rung, Eron lifted me up, wrapping his arm around my waist as we headed across the surface of Telvin. I glanced over my shoulder to where Jane was still standing, peering down anxiously.

I wrenched away from Eron, sprinting for Jane, the gravity on the surface of Telvin allowing me to move with ease. "You can't wait until everyone is up. You need to get to The Pittsburgh now."

Jane didn't look at me. "Always worrying. I'm not waiting for everyone, just my crew. Not that I'd take off without as many of these poor souls as possible, but my family is what matters to me. Now get out of here. I'll be right behind you as soon as Masha and Dar are up. None of us are going anywhere without Masha anyhow."

The top of Dar's head popped into the light, Xia draped over one shoulder, Tia over the other. I stared in amazement, hardly believing what my eyes were showing me. Dar was big and strong, parts of his body made from Gartian grade alloy, but climbing the ladder with two children thrown over his shoulders was a feat I hadn't expected possible with the awkwardness of it.

Eron spun me around, dragging me off. "Waste of energy to save them. We're all going to regret it later."

"Everyone deserves a second chance."

"No. Nobody does. Not them, and especially not me."

I stumbled, my feet dragging a bit as Eron continued pulling me along. "And yet you had no problem with the idea of taking me and running off. Why was that different? What changed?"

When our ship came into view, we picked up the pace, clambering into the open airlock. It was a bit disconcerting only being able to see the inside of the ship since the rest of it was cloaked. I didn't understand the technology, but was thankful for it.

Dropping down in front of me, Eron unzipped my suit, his lavender gaze snagging mine. "I lived in constant darkness for so long. When you showed up, you were like a sun, burning so brightly that I simply wanted to bask in your warmth and light. It felt like you could keep away the darkness forever, and I wanted that. All of it. But then I realized it was selfish." He offered me his hand so I could step out of the space suit. My T-shirt and pants were plastered to my body with sweat. The sudden chill caused goose bumps to erupt in quick succession along my flesh.

Wrapping my arms around my middle, I swayed towards Eron. "If it's what you need, I'll be your light. It's not selfish. I want you to be with me just as much as you want to be with me. Leaving me, pulling away, constantly telling me how you don't deserve a second chance ..." My throat closed, and the rest of my words lodged there. I grabbed Eron, yanking him against me. The material of the space suit was rough against my skin, the smell of it musty. "I don't care what you've done, or what you say, I'll never let you go. Never."

His hands slid down my back, kneading gently. "I don't want to snuff out your light. You've been around me for such a short period of time and look what's happened already."

"The creature, all of him, had to die. I feel no regret over what I did."

"Which means you're already changing. Before we left here, you healed one of him, you couldn't help yourself."

"We all make mistakes."

Dar's steady footsteps clinked up the ramp into the airlock, Masha's tread pinging right along with it. "I'm going to check on my engine!" Masha rushed past me, her black eyes wide with panic.

"My ship, *my* engine!" Jane called after her, a grin on her face.

I chuckled. "I don't think she heard you."

"Oh, she always hears me, she pretends not to. Just like she pretends to be all child-like and innocent."

Dar shifted the twins on his shoulders, grimacing slightly. "Where do you want me to put them?"

"Medical wing," I said, taking note of how Eron had melted into the background, his expression neutral as he stared at the twins. "Strap them down. Just to be safe." I stepped forward, checking their energy levels. "They should be awake soon." I nibbled on the inside of my cheek, coming to a decision. I yanked a bit of energy from each of them, assuring they'd stay unconscious for just a little while longer. I wanted to be able to take care of our new guests before dealing with Xia and Tia.

"I think that's everyone." Jane stabbed her index finger into the button to close the airlock. "I'm going to go see if Masha thinks we're good to go, or if work needs to be done." She strode off, mumbling under her breath.

Motioning to our guests, I backed up slowly, waving at them to follow me. I glanced over at Eron, who hadn't moved. "I'm going to need your help healing them. And with getting as many as them fitted with translator implants as possible."

He nodded, his expression unwavering. "Whatever you need."

AS IT TURNED OUT, The Pittsburgh's upside-down status hadn't caused any damage to its machinery, and righting it was merely a matter of actually knowing how to pilot the ship, thank the stars. Once it was safely off of Telvin, and hurtling towards Gartian territory, Eron and I set to work on healing our guests. A few—like tiger-man—were unscathed in any way, but with most that wasn't the case. Some injuries weren't obvious things, but on closer inspection, the horrors of treatment on Telvin came to light. Not that I wasn't personally well acquainted.

"She's blind in one eye." I waved my hand in front of a large, feathered humanoid. I would have never known by simply looking at her wide-set, beautiful, azure eyes.

Nothing on the surface appeared unusual. "What purpose would they have to blind her?"

"It was a means to an end." Eron hovered behind me, watching my work, but not interfering since some of our guests seemed to know him, which wasn't a good thing.

"Did you—" I gulped. "Did you do this?"

"Yes."

"Why?"

Eron brushed a hand down the back of my arm, leaning in so I could feel his body heat. "They wanted to know—"

"Never mind. I don't want any details. What's done is done. Let's just fix what we can and move forward."

"It's permanent, or I would have healed it, just so I could do it again. You remember how it worked there."

I did. All too well. Shuddering, I pushed memories away, his and mine, before they could resurface. "Hand me a set of translators." Eron pressed them into my open palm, and I held them in front of the female's good eye, tapping behind one of my ears.

She nodded and said, "Yes, I understand. I'm ready."

Tilting her head to the side, I made the appropriate incision, placing the translator where it needed to go, and then did the same on the other side. "How's that?"

She smiled with relief. "Oh, I can understand you. I forgot what it's like. Thank you."

"Of course. Now, if you could please wait outside, Jane will be along soon to direct you where to go."

She jumped off the table, taking my hands within hers,

her brightly colored rainbow feathers brushing against my skin. "Thank you! Thank you for everything!"

My chest bloomed with warmth. Gratitude wasn't why I healed, but I would be lying if I said I didn't enjoy it just a bit. What did make healing such a blessing was knowing how I could help mend things broken by cruelty from nature and other beings. I could make a positive difference, no matter how small, to work towards making the Universe a better place.

"Tamzea," Jane called from the door. "I need to see you."

I glanced around at all the eager waiting faces, some filled with pain as well. "I'm kind of busy at the moment."

"Eron, you take over for a bit. I need Tamzea for something important."

Eron grabbed my arm, a scowl tugging his lips down. "I can't. Don't leave me alone with them."

"Maybe they realize your hand was forced when it came to what you did on Telvin. After all, you did aid in their rescue."

His jaw muscles worked, his teeth grinding together. "I'm not … my healing abilities are weak at best. Sometimes I can't even manage to access them."

I grabbed the side of his face, narrowing my eyes. "I don't want to hear your excuses anymore. Just do it. Heal them. You have the power. I can feel it burning within you."

Before he could say anything else, Jane yanked me away from him, tugging me into the hallway. "Look, I didn't want to freak anyone out with panicked talk since most of them can't understand me, but I need you."

"What is it?"

"Something is wrong with my mate mark. Something serious."

I heaved an annoyed sigh, dragging my feet. "Come on, Jane. You can't be serious about this. Again? With everything that's going on … again with the mate mark thing?"

Right there in the hall, Jane ripped her shirt off, leaving her upper body naked. She pivoted so her back was facing me, her arms waving in panic. "Tell me now you still believe I'm overreacting or imagining things."

Mesmerized, I glided my fingers over the intricate pattern, half of it black, the skin appearing deadened. The energy of it was off, murky, and slow. I swallowed around the lump in my throat. "He's— Ash is dying." I wasn't sure how I knew, but I did, I just knew.

I'd expected Jane to break down completely, to cry, to scream out in rage or anguish, but she remained perfectly still, her voice even and calm. "I see. Well, I'm not going to let that happen." She tugged her shirt on with jerky movements. "I'm leaving immediately. You're in charge until I get back."

"What? No! I can't be captain of this ship, even if it's temporary. You know I can't handle—"

Jane grabbed me by the shoulders, her face a mask of determination. "You're going to do it because I need you to. We all need you to. If he's dying," she flicked her gaze away, anguish swirling in her gaze, "I don't have any time to waste. But we have to go after Zula, and we have to get all of those people to the Gartian territory so we can figure out how to get them back to their respective homes. There's too much—it's too much. And I need you to be able to handle this."

So many thoughts were running rampant through my mind. But one stood out clearer than the others. *What wouldn't you do for Eron?* Jane had to go after Ash, she didn't have a choice, and I couldn't let my insecurities inadvertently cause his death. I would never forgive myself. I notched my chin up, steeling myself mentally. "I'll handle it." *Somehow.*

"Thank you." She turned into her flame form, streaking down the hallway, leaving a trace of smoke in her wake.

I won't let you down. I promise.

Chapter 23

You're in charge now, don't mess it up. Part of being a good leader was knowing when to delegate, and to prioritize.

Marching into the engine room, I spotted Dar and Masha locked in a passionate embrace. I coughed into my fist, hating that I had to interrupt their reunion. "Jane's gone and I'm in charge until she gets back."

"Where'd she go?" Masha's face scrunched up with concern.

"Ash is dying ..." I fidgeted, wishing what I'd said wasn't the truth. Jane had been right about something being wrong all along. She should have trusted her instincts instead of relying on me. I can only sense certain things, and apparently couldn't get a read on the mate mark until it was almost too late.

"Her mate mark ..." I shook my head and cleared my throat. "It doesn't matter. She's going to save him and it'll all be fine. In the meantime, I'm going to need you to be in charge of flying The Pittsburgh."

"We're already flying her." Masha's lower lip stuck out in anticipation of what I was about to say.

A lot of times the autopilot could be counted on when we were simply cruising, but at the moment someone needed to oversee things in case something went wrong. "You need to be up in the control room. You need to take over for Jane and Zula."

"But my engine—"

Dar placed his hand on her shoulder, addressing me. "Consider it done."

"Thanks. I'm going to go back and help Eron with our guests. Let me know when we reach Gartian territory."

I spun on my heel, heading back to the medical wing. *Okay, step one taken care of.* Next, I needed to help Eron with the rest of the injured and get our guests off our ship. From there the Gartians would aid them. Then, depending on when Jane got back, we might have to go after Zula without her. Which reminded me that I had to view the surveillance records Jane had taken from Telvin.

I switched directions and headed to the control room, where I was sure Jane had left what I needed to search for clues of Zula's whereabouts. Eron would just have to deal with our patients without me for a little longer. I hadn't felt any spike in anxiety through our bond, so I figured he was fine for the time being.

Okay, as long as things don't go horribly wrong, or go— The twins! How could I have forgotten about the twins? They needed to be dealt with, too. I switched directions again, knowing I had to figure out what to do with Xia and Tia before anything else.

I burst into the other side of the medical wing, where Xia and Tia were being kept. Panting, I bent over to catch my breath.

"Have you come to kill us?"

I whipped my head up, surprised that Xia was awake. Her tiny face was turned towards me, no fear evident in her expression despite her question. "No, of course not. Why would you think that?" Tia appeared to still be unconscious.

"Because of what we did to you, and all the others."

I waved my hands around Xia, checking her energy against Tia's. It was the same and yet one sister was awake and the other slept. "You're stronger than her."

"Just a bit. Not anywhere it matters though. It's not like with you and our father. You're matched perfectly."

I perched on the edge of a cot, not sure of what to do next. "It's different for every Metza pair."

"If you're not going to kill us, then what are you going to do?"

"I'm not sure yet."

"It would be simpler if you did kill us. I don't understand why you're not going to."

I was taken aback. She was discussing her and her sister's possible demise like she was telling me she'd seen a shooting star recently. "Do you want to die?"

"Not really."

"So what do you want?"

"For you to die."

Chills ran up my spine. "Why?"

Xia stared at me, her face scrunching up. "Because our father hates us and it's your fault."

"Killing me would only make him hate you more." If I could just reason with Xia, and Tia, too, then maybe I could figure out how to get through to them in the long run.

"He'll never love us now so it doesn't matter. We just want to make him suffer more."

My head swam, spots dancing in front of my eyes. I blinked Xia back into focus. "Maybe if you acted differently you both could mend your relationship with him."

"It's too late for that," she said, a smug smile twisting her lips.

"No! Stop! Get away from them!" Eron grabbed me around the waist, yanking me off the cot. "She's stealing your energy and you're not able to guard against it." He cradled me to his chest as he backed away, glaring at Xia.

I did a quick assessment, realizing what he said was true. I couldn't believe I hadn't noticed. "It'll be fine. Now that I know I can put up a shield." But hadn't I thought that before?

"No." He stalked from the room with me still in his arms. "They're not normal. I'm the only one who can block them. It's one of the other reasons they kept me around at Telvin."

Xia giggled, calling after us, "He's right. Tia and I used to scare them."

My eyes widened. "How is that possible? You're my Metza, so if you can block them I should be able to. Plus, normal Mazatimz—"

"I told you, they're not normal. They're abominations."

If that were true, then there'd be no place for them. They wouldn't be accepted by our people, or any other for that matter. "Oh. I just thought …" I choked back a sob, tears erupting from my eyes. I didn't think of Xia and Tia as my children. My discovery of them had been too sudden for attachment when they'd been hell-bent on killing me from the beginning. But on some level, I imagined helping them, rehabilitating them, and then one day we could all be a family.

"Shh … Tamzy, please. I can't stand it when you cry." Eron brushed his lips against my forehead, lingering.

"I wanted us to be a family. I knew it could take a while, but I thought eventually …" I sobbed into his shirt, wanting to disappear. I couldn't seem to stop being naïve about these things. Intellectually I knew I was acting silly, but my heart wanted it, all of it.

"You can't allow yourself to think of them as our children. I warned you. They have our DNA, but they're something else. I don't know why they turned out the way they did, but … But, Tamzy, they can't be allowed to live."

Digging my fingers into his back, I pressed my face harder into his chest. "No! You don't mean that. They're just children."

We'd arrived at my living quarters, the journey in Eron's arms keeping me from noticing where we'd been heading. He placed me on my bed, following me down. He cupped my face, his thumbs sweeping along my cheeks. "Those two girls are the closest thing to evil I've ever come across. And yes, they're only children, their abilities still developing. But what happens when they come into their full powers and their taste for blood heightens right along with it? How will you feel about all the innocent lives that have and will be lost?"

"I can't do it, Eron. I just can't."

He pulled away from me, staring down at the snake on his forearm. "Let me do it for you. No matter how hard you try to deny it, I know what I've become, what I am. Use me. I want you to … need you to."

"No! There has to be another way." But if what he said was true … And I had no reason to think he'd ever lie to me about such a thing. *No … no … no.*

"There's not. They're a creation of Telvin, made into a weapon. There's nowhere we can take or send them that'll be safe. And what if the Denards get a hold of them again? What if—"

"Okay," I croaked, pressing my face into my pillow. Rage tunneled its way through my body, causing me to tremble. All of it was Telvin's, or really, the Denard's fault.

"Okay to what? You'll let me take care of them?"

I nodded into my pillow, the material damp from my tears. I couldn't bring myself to say the words, though. It was as if I managed to respond without words I was somehow removed from the situation, that the decision wasn't mine anymore and had nothing to do with me. Which wasn't fair to Eron. I pushed myself up, meeting his gaze, and swiped at my runny nose. "Okay, I want you to take care of them."

He pulled me into his arms, squeezing me tight. I inhaled his spicy scent, wishing I could lose myself in him entirely. He kissed the top of my head, and disentangled himself from me, leaving me bereft without his heat. Careful not to meet my gaze, he left my quarters without another word.

I stared after him, hot, angry tears sliding down my cheeks, my body shaking uncontrollably. I was too unfocused to stabilize myself, too distraught to feel Eron through our bond. I'd never felt so helpless before, not even when I'd been at Telvin.

Telvin. Damn you. Damn you for everything you've done.

Chapter 24

Seconds trickled into minutes, minutes into hours. And still, I waited for Eron to return. I didn't know how he planned on snuffing out the lives of Xia and Tia, and a part of me didn't want to ever know, but as time slipped away horrible images assaulted my mind. Images that weren't limited to the deaths of the twins.

What if they somehow overpowered him? What if something went wrong and Eron's dead? No, I would feel it, wouldn't I? Unless I'm too distraught already ... No. It's not possible. Everything will be fine.

Pacing across my living quarters, I paused every so often to stare at the door. *Come on. What's taking you so long?* Finally reaching my breaking point, I hurried into the hallway, running headlong into Eron, who appeared to have been standing outside my door. *How didn't I sense him?*

His head was hung, his body tense, and he remained perfectly still as if he didn't want to acknowledge me for some reason. I touched his arm, and he jerked away from me, backing up a few steps.

"Eron? What happened?"

"I let you down." His voice was thick with shame, making me want to comfort him. But when I reached for him, he backed up until he hit the opposite wall. "I let you down," he said again.

"Just tell me what happened."

He lifted his head, his eyes wild. "I already told you. I let you down."

I ground my teeth together, resisting the urge to yell. He was driving me absolutely batty. "I'll be the judge of that. Now, tell me what happened."

Eron's head dropped again, his chin resting on his chest. "I went to see them. I wasn't sure how I was going to do … it. I just knew I had to … for you." He swallowed, his Adam's apple bobbing up and down. "I finally decided to suck all of their lifeforce from them, that way it would be like they were going to sleep. It would have been easy, painless." His fist hit the wall, causing me to jump. "But then Tia looked at me. She looked at me—she looked at me and I couldn't do it. All I did was put them into a deep sleep." A sob broke free from Eron's chest. "So you see, I let you down."

I made no conscious effort to move. One moment I was standing a few feet away, and the next I was wrapping my arms around his waist. He collapsed against me, silent sobs shaking his body. It was the most emotion I'd felt from him since our reunion. Tangled up within regret and sorrow was the old Eron, *my* Eron. He wasn't irrevocably altered after all, just buried beneath shame and guilt and a host of other dark emotions.

"Shh …" I stroked his hair, stumbling across the hall towards my quarters. "It's okay. Everything is going to be okay."

"No. It's not. Nothing will ever be okay again."

"Yes, it will." Even though we were back at square one with the twins, warmth bloomed within me. I'd never turn away from Eron, no matter what happened. I loved him unconditionally. But the fact that he was unable to kill two children, even if they needed to die … it filled me with relief.

I settled on my bed with Eron, cradling him to me, his head resting on my chest as he continued to silently sob. "You didn't let me down. As long as you don't try to leave me again, you'll never let me down."

"I don't deserve you anymore." His words were muffled against my chest.

"Again, let me be the judge of that."

"I wanted to protect you, from all of it. Even when we were kids I wanted to protect you from anything that could hurt you. You've always been the more sensitive one and because of it I knew I had to protect you."

It was true. Harsh words hurt my feelings, and others suffering didn't just bother me, it ripped me to the core. Eron had known that and tried to shield me from life's hardships. It was an impossible task, but I loved him that much more for it.

Smiling, I pulled away from him enough so I could plant a kiss on both of his eyelids. "We're supposed to protect each other. And you've done enough. You've been through enough. It's my turn to protect you, to heal you from the things Telvin put you through. Remember, together we can do anything."

"I've done too many horrible things. Maybe I don't deserve peace. I should have done more. Fought harder. Everything is my fault. Maybe I don't—"

Taking him by the shoulders, I shook him as hard as I was able. His eyes widened in surprise. "I'm not doing this again. This is the last time I'm going to say this to you so you better listen carefully. You're not tainted. You haven't become poisonous like the snake on your arm. You're my Eron, and yes, you're a bit broken right now, confused and sad, but I will fix you."

"I've taken so many lives, caused so much pain …" He pulled away from me, his gaze blankly fixing on the floor. "I can't close my eyes without seeing them. And not just at night. Every waking moment I'm haunted. All those innocent lives. So much blood. There's so much blood on my hands and I'll never be able to get it out.

"You can't continue to shoulder the blame for things you were forced to do on Telvin. Instead, spend the rest of your life healing like you were meant to do. Wash away the blood of those innocents with good deeds."

"I can't. I tried. It's not in me like it used to be."

Surprise raced through me. "You didn't heal our guests?"

"No." The word hung in the air between us, thick with implications.

"Oh, well ..." What could I do if he refused to try? There was nothing wrong with his abilities physically. His problems all lay between his ears. "Get up," I commanded. "You're going to go heal them now. I'll help you."

Eron grimaced before rolling away from me. "I can't deal with another failure right now."

Grabbing his shoulder, I spun him towards me, glaring down at him. "We're going to send the twins to our people. I thought it was a mistake before, but I've changed my mind. Let them take on the burden. Xia and Tia won't be able to harm the elders like they so easily can others." *Probably.* "The elders owe us that much after letting us be taken and never coming for us. In fact, they owe us that and a lot more. And if they banish them, or worse, so be it. We'll deal with the consequences later. I'll give Dar instructions on what to do. I'll draw up a document explaining what happened, and send it with them. We'll put them in a pod, and off they go. Our people will shoulder the responsibility of unmaking the deadly weapon Telvin created with our DNA."

Eron remained silent so I continued. "But first we're going to march into the medical wing, and you're going to heal our guests."

"I can't," he croaked.

"Yes, you can," I growled, yanking him to his feet. I dug

my nails into his forearm, dragging him after me, although he didn't put up much of a fight.

All heads whipped towards us when we entered the medical wing, hope flaring in some creatures' eyes, hate directed at Eron in others. Releasing Eron, I stepped into the middle of the room, hands on my hips. I met each individual gaze head-on, attempting to communicate that I meant business.

"All right. I know most of you can't understand me. But maybe you'll get the gist of what I'm saying. We're here to help you, both of us." I motioned for Eron to come to me. I took his hand within mine, squeezing it gently. "He was as much a prisoner at Telvin as all of you. He was forced to do things that he never would have done if he had the choice. You won't blame him."

People shifted, tension palpable in the air. "They don't understand you," Eron whispered.

"Doesn't matter. I just said it for me."

I plastered a warm smile on my face, waving a Guaviva forward. He was less tentative, probably because Masha had been able to explain things to them. After checking him over, I sent a pulse of healing energy into him, mending the small contusions on his arm. I then motioned for him to sit down so I could insert his translators.

When we were done, I patted him on the head, unable to resist. "All right. There you go."

He threw his arms around me, dangling from my neck as he showed his appreciation in a child-like hug. "Thank you! It's so good to be able to understand more than my kind again."

I knew Guavivas weren't children, or built like them, but I still reacted as if a child was hugging me. I clutched him to me tightly before setting him gently on his feet. "What's your name?"

"Rio."

I hunched down, bringing myself to his eye level. "Nice to officially meet you, Rio. I'm Tamzea. And I was wondering if you could do me a small favor to show your appreciation."

"Name it," he said.

"I'm not sure the extent of what Masha was able to explain to you, but Eron," I motioned behind me, "he was a prisoner on Telvin, too. The thing is, as a Mazatimz, what they did to him, forcing him to torture, well it's … how can I put this … it would be like someone forcing Masha to damage her engine."

Rio gasped, his face twisted in horror. "A Guaviva would never purposely damage their chosen machine."

"But what if it came down to hurting their chosen machine, and protecting the one they love most in the world?"

Rio glanced at Eron, understanding and pity moving through his black gaze. "I see. And why are you telling me this?"

"Because Eron was forced to do the equivalent of damaging his chosen machine for the past decade. Now he's a bit ... broken. And I need to fix him. Can you please help me fix him?"

Rio glanced at Eron again and then nodded. "I'll do what I can. Masha spoke of how good the crew of this ship is to her. She told us how she loves all of you as much as her engine."

I knew that was a big compliment coming from a Guaviva and it brought a smile to my face. "Eron needs to find himself in his healing ability again. He's lost what it means to be a Mazatimz, and I want him to heal everyone here, starting with the other Guavivas. Will you speak to them for me? Explain that he means them no harm and that he only wants to help. Explain it all. Please."

"Yes, I will explain to them what you just told me." He motioned to the other Guavivas to gather around as he approached them. His voice dropped to a level where I couldn't quite make out what he was saying.

"Just because they agree to let me heal them doesn't mean I'll be able to do it," Eron said.

"I have a feeling you're having problems because you sense the mistrust in your would-be patients. Once Rio explains, that won't be there. And then once you heal all the Guavivas, the rest of them will see your intentions." I grabbed his hand, squeezing. "It'll work. I know it will."

"And if it doesn't?"

"It will."

He pulled me into his side, kissing my temple tenderly, his hot breath washing along my cheek. "I love how no matter what happens, your default setting is always optimism."

"They'll do it," Rio exclaimed, rushing towards us. "They're no longer afraid of your Eron. They understand why he did what he did to some of them."

I dropped down to give Rio a quick hug. "Thank you. This means a lot to me."

"It's nothing."

"It isn't nothing. It's a lot." Standing, I motioned to the exam table. "I'll need you to translate for the time being. Now, tell whoever wants to go first to get up on the table."

"Dorma, get up on the exam table and the male Mazatimz will take care of you."

A Guaviva with blonde hair and a slight limp hesitantly made her way to the table. I lifted her up and gave her a pleasant smile. "Come on, Eron. She's ready."

Eron trudged over to stand next to me, his head hung and shoulders hunched. "I don't want you to get your hopes up."

"Eron, please. I need you to try, to really try."

He lifted his head, anger flashing in his eyes. "You think I didn't try before?"

Dorma shifted away from Eron ever so slightly, the tone of his voice startling her. I glanced at Rio. "Tell Dorma not to be nervous. Eron's just upset because he's having difficulties connecting with his healing abilities."

Rio informed Dorma what was going on, and she noticeably relaxed. Her large black eyes moved over Eron as she brazenly studied him. "I'm not afraid. I understand now. They tortured you, too." She touched Eron gently on the back of his hand.

Eron's eyes widened, something akin to hope replacing the anger that was there a moment ago. He shuffled forward, his expression intense. His lips curled up slightly as he patted Dorma affectionately on the head. "I hope I can help you. I want to help you."

Rio repeated to Dorma what Eron said, and she smiled sweetly. "I know you'll be able to help me."

Eron raised his hands, moving them stiffly through the air, assessing her energy. I stepped behind him, not wanting him to see me doing the same. My plan was to aid him so he could help Dorma. I had no doubt Eron would be able to heal with no limitations if he just got his confidence back.

Through our bond, while Eron was working with Dorma, I stumbled upon a block within Eron's energies. His power was building up behind it, pushing, but not able to break through, only the smallest of traces trickling around it. I'd been right. He had all the power necessary to heal, but no access to it.

"It's not working," Eron grated. "I'm not healing her."

"Keep trying." Pushing my energy down the line, I put pressure on the block, imagining my power moving with Eron's through the block and obliterating it. *Please, please, please.* But it was as if the block fought back, resisting both of us. *We're Metzas. We can do this. Together we can do this.* My eyes slid shut, and I gritted my teeth, putting everything I had behind breaking that damn block.

"Tamzy, I can't." Eron's voice sounded far away. Almost too far away.

"Keep trying," I heard myself say, my voice strained.

Please, please, please. White light exploded behind my eyes, and I staggered back, temporarily blinded. But I wouldn't let up. I kept pushing my energy into Eron, determined to heal him.

My limbs tingled, and my knees gave out. Another explosion of light flashed behind my closed eyes.

Eron screamed out in agony.

My body went numb, and I fell into darkness for a moment, before being yanked into blindingly white light. My eyes widened, taking in the scene in front of me. Eron stood with his arms thrown wide, golden energy surging through the air from him, surrounding all of those who were injured. Pure joy flooded from our bond, a peace settling over me.

Eron's healing everyone. Eron's healing everyone and it's the most beautiful thing I've ever seen.

A grin stretched across my face even as exhaustion caused me to slump forward. I tried to hold on, peering up at Eron from my prone position, not wanting to miss a single second of what was happening. Unfortunately, my body had other ideas.

Chapter 25

"Tamzy. My Tamzy. Wake up."

I groaned, entirely too comfortable to move. "Don't wanna," I mumbled. "Go away."

Soft kisses pressed along my face, causing me to stretch in delight. I inhaled Eron's spicy scent, smiling to myself. "Hold me. Just hold me for a little while longer."

"Tamzy. You need to wake up. We've just entered Gartian territory, and we need our captain."

Everything came flooding back to me, and I jolted up, nearly banging my forehead into Eron's chin. "How long was I out? And what happened after I lost consciousness?"

Eron grinned at me, his countenance light and airy, joy dancing in his beautiful eyes. "I healed them. I healed all of them." He wrapped his arms around me, burying his face in my hair. "You did it. You fixed me."

I gasped, tears bursting from my eyes. "Oh, Eron! I can't … I just—" I couldn't find the words to express how happy I was. Or maybe words simply didn't exist for how I felt in that moment. I'd witnessed the beginning of the miracle before I'd lost consciousness, but until he confirmed it, until I saw the joy in his eyes, I didn't fully believe it.

"All of them, Tamzy. And all of them at once. Only the most powerful of our kind have ever been able to do such a thing. And I couldn't have done any of it without you."

I have him back. I can feel it. I finally have him back. "I told you we could do anything together."

"Yes, you did." His fingers dug into my flesh with the edge of pain, and his arms squeezed tight enough to make it difficult to breathe, but I didn't care.

I reveled in the moment, never wanting it to end. I had the other half of my soul back, the love of my life, and for just a second I wanted to pretend there would be no more hardships in our future. I wanted to exist only in our current joy. For I may have fixed Eron's ability to heal others, but the road to his recovery was far from over. I couldn't merely erase his memories of his time on Telvin with a concentration of energy, no matter how much I wished I could.

"We'll be landing as soon as I'm directed to a port," Dar's voice crackled over the intercom.

I disentangled myself reluctantly from Eron. "I guess we'll have to catch up later." We'd been together sexually several times since our reunion, but I couldn't wait to be intimate with Eron now that the biggest piece of his baggage was gone.

As I straightened my clothes, I caught him glaring down at the snake on his arm. "I can take care of it for you." I ran my fingers over it, tracing the raised skin.

He snatched his arm away. "No. I want to keep it. I want to remember."

I worried the inside of my cheek, considering his words. "I don't think you'll ever forget. Although I wish you would. You don't need the snake to remember."

"No. Every creature is the grand sum of everything they've experienced in their lives. Every little bit is there. Who I am today, and who I'll be tomorrow, and the day after, is shaped by all of my past experiences. I don't want to forget the ones that nearly destroyed me."

I stared down at the snake, hating it just a little. It was a symbol of all the things I wished I could have saved him from. "I don't like it."

He slid his arms around me, bowing me back, his gaze boring into mine. "It's who I am now. And I do remember you telling me it could symbolize transmutation. It can serve as both a reminder of what I never want to be again, and how even that can be morphed into something good ... in the end. And you don't need to worry about me backsliding anymore—about me losing myself. It's like a fog from my brain has been lifted, and a darkness from my heart obliterated. I am a Mazatimz again, truly."

He was right. I'd told him the self-inflicted branding could represent something positive if he just changed his attitude towards it. "I meant what I said, it's just," I paused while I gathered my thoughts, "it reminds me how we were separated for all those years. It reminds us how different in so many ways we are now."

"Our souls are still a perfect fit."

"I know, it's just ..." What was it? What about it was bothering me so much when it hadn't before? Maybe it was because he saw the snake as a reminder of how far he'd fallen while he was at Telvin, and I hadn't been with him. I'd abandoned him. If he was going to keep the snake, I deserved a mark just like his to remind me of how I shouldn't have given up. *I should never give up. At least not on Eron. I'll never make that mistake again.*

"If you refuse to heal that mark, I want one, too. I want one just like it."

Eron's lip curled back in a snarl. "Why? Or are you attempting to manipulate me to remove it?"

"No, I'm not trying to manipulate you. I want a reminder, too. I want to remember that no matter how far gone one of us seems to be, we'll transmute that dark energy and heal ... together. Sappy maybe, stupid definitely. But I want it. It'll make me feel better if we both have that mark. It'll be the symbol of our Metza pair."

He chuckled in disbelief. "You're one of a kind, that's for sure."

"Thanks?"

"It's a good thing, I promise." He kissed the tip of my nose. "No one else, no matter how powerful of a Mazatimz, could have done what you did. And I doubt any would have even tried."

The Pittsburgh's lights dimmed, signaling our landing.

"We need to be on and off the Gartian planet as quickly as possible. The longer we wait to go after Zula, the less chance we have of finding her."

"Have you had the opportunity to look over the surveillance feed Jane left for you?"

"No." I strode out into the hallway. "Other things kept getting in the way, but it wasn't like I could do anything about it until we dropped off our guests." I also secretly hoped Jane would show up with Ash in tow before I had to lead the mission to find Zula. I would do it, but I was concerned if we needed brute force to rescue her that I'd be little to no good.

As we made our way towards the airlock, where we'd be exiting The Pittsburgh, different species wandered the halls, some of them a bit bewildered. We hadn't had enough translators, so not everyone knew what was going on.

I waved at several furry creatures, their faces humanoid, their bodies short and squat, motioning for them to follow us. They waddled along, hope filling their eyes. It was amazing how many unfamiliar species Telvin had taken prisoner, especially because, as a Mazatimz, I had a wide knowledge of all the most prevalent species in the Universe. *What was Telvin's endgame?*

Dar appeared beside us, clomping along in our wake. "Yarza has requested a meeting with everyone, the ex-prisoners of Telvin included, after all are fitted with translators. Until then, he wishes to ask if you require any other services?"

"I need someone to have a look at the surveillance feed Jane left for us from Telvin. I hope to get a clue where Zula is, but I also want to see if there's anything else helpful to aid our cause on them. There's probably other useful information we could use."

"Where did Jane leave the disk?"

"Control room."

Dar nodded once. "I will take care of it."

Masha darted around the corner, a broad smile on her face. "I love this place! If I didn't love my engine so much I'd want to stay here forever!" She jumped up and down, clapping.

"Calm down, we can't be here long. We have to find Zula."

Masha's smile faded around the edges. "I know."

I had no idea what to make of it. Masha cared about Zula, and about all of us, but sometimes it was as if machines and Dar were the only things she wanted to put an effort into. Of course, Dar was half machine himself. I rolled my eyes. Guavivas were strange creatures.

Grabbing Eron's hand, who had been suspiciously silent, I tugged him along after me. "I need to get some food in me before the meeting. And don't think I'm going to forget about what we were talking about earlier."

He grimaced. "I wouldn't be so lucky."

As we exited the ship, we were greeted by four Gartians, two of which were Dar's brothers. They escorted us to our temporary lodging, where we could shower and order food. Eron stared in amazement at everything, having never been on the Gartian planet before. I wondered if he had preconceived ideas about it like I used to.

The Gartians used their fierce reputation to keep unwanted visitors out of their territory. It was the Denards who infected their population with the G-Pox, which forced them to turn themselves into cyborgs in order to survive. Not many knew what the Gartians even looked like, assuming they were half-rotted lunatics who couldn't even bother to name their planet. They merely wanted to keep prying eyes out so they could plan their revenge, which Ash was an integral part of.

But what if Ash dies? No. I can't let myself think that. If Ash dies, it will destroy Jane. He was her bonded phoenix mate and the only male she'd ever loved.

My mind kept cycling through everything I needed to take care of. I didn't know how Jane managed to be captain and polish off firejuice the way she did. *Huh. Maybe being captain is why she drinks so much.*

Eron tapped his fork against mine. "You haven't touched your food. And your mind is elsewhere. Let me help."

I blinked, registering that I'd somehow ended up at a table with heaps of food in front of me, a fork in my hand, and all of it set up in our temporary quarters. The last thing I remembered clearly was being escorted from The Pittsburgh … *Huh.*

Stabbing what appeared to be some kind of fruit, I

waved it in the air. "Did you remember to give the note to Dar? You know, the one to be sent with Xia and Tia?"

"Yes, of course, I remembered."

Chewing, I barely tasted the food. "And you gave them enough sedative to keep them knocked out for the entire trip?"

"Yes. I took care of everything while you recharged after healing me. The twins should already be on their way."

I poked around my plate, not as hungry as I thought I was. "Do you think we did the right thing with them?"

Eron placed his hand over mine. "We did our best."

"Mmm …" I pushed away from the table. "I didn't want them to die, but if I'm being honest with myself, I felt no motherly bond with them. I wanted to, though—had hoped to eventually."

"They weren't our children. Not really."

"That's not how it works, Eron. They have our DNA, it doesn't matter how they came about—they're ours."

Eron shoved away from the small table, his chair toppling to the ground. "If you'd seen all the horrible things they've done …" He slammed his fist into the wall. "They enjoyed killing. It sickened me."

"Maybe it wasn't the killing itself that they enjoyed. Maybe it was the praise or the feeling of power, I don't know, but it's all out of our hands now. I'm sorry I brought it up. They're gone and we have other things to concentrate on. Like finding Zula."

"You want to see if they've pulled the footage from Telvin up yet?"

"Yes." My food suddenly forgotten, just like so many other things, I headed for the door.

LEANING OVER ZAR'S SHOULDER—AT least I think it was Zar—I alternated between squinting and widening my eyes. "That can't be right. It doesn't make sense. Play the last part again."

Zar rewound the footage, replaying the part that astounded me. Zula had been freed by a Talsen, one that had access to the codes to her room, and then she willingly boarded an escape pod with him.

Why did she leave without Masha and where did she go? Who exactly is the Talsen?

He was huge, larger than any Talsen I'd seen before. Even his muscles had muscles. *Why would Zula just go with him like that?* I was missing something. I'd been sure of it the first time I'd watched the footage, and now several times later, I wasn't any closer to figuring it out. *Damn it.*

"I'm not sure what the make and model of that particular pod is, so I won't be much help," Eron said, frustration evident in his tone.

I patted his hand. "It's fine. We'll run the stills through the database on The Pittsburgh. We have programs for this type of thing. It comes in handy for tracking down bounties."

"We have it, too," Zar declared with indignation. "What kind of primitives do you take us for?"

"Umm ... none. I didn't take the Gartians for any kind of primitive. I just wasn't thinking. I'm under a lot of stress. I'm sorry if I insulted you." Zar grunted. I was used to dealing with Dar who had become friendlier from his time on our ship. Zar may be identical in appearance to Dar, but he certainly had a grumpier disposition.

Zar tilted his head as if listening to something, then flipped off the monitor, and stood. "Yarza is calling the meeting to order. I will show you the way." He stalked off, obviously expecting us to follow.

Sighing heavily, I scurried after him, but my mind was lost in thoughts of Zula. *Why would she leave with that Talsen? And where is she now?*

Chapter 26

All talking halted when Yarza, the leader of the Gartians, entered the meeting room. I'd only met him once before, and it'd been in a meeting much like the one that was about to begin. Yarza was larger than Dar and his brothers, but also more intimidating. He had the kind of commanding presence only truly great leaders possess. His face was made almost completely of Gartian grade alloy, as was his entire left arm. His dark blue eyes were humanoid, filled with untold pain and sorrow, which tugged at my heartstrings. The suffering he himself must have experienced, along with witnessing it amongst his people ... I wondered if at any point someone like me could have helped in any small way.

Yarza flexed his metal arm and began to speak. His voice filled the room, making everyone sit up straighter. "It was not too long ago that we invited Captain Jane

Wexis and her crew from The Pittsburgh to be our allies. With the help of Ash, one of the last remaining phoenixes, our goal is to exact revenge on the Denards and to free the Universe from their tyranny. Our first step was to spread the word far and wide to every planet, every star, and every species and settlement so that none are unprepared when the UGFS and the Denards retaliate. The task promised to be a slow one," he raised his hands palm up, and smiled, the expression menacing, "but now it's gotten a bit easier, thanks to all of you."

He motioned to the prisoners from Telvin. "You must go back to your people and share with them the atrocities which were done to you by the Denards. You must share it far and wide. The people of this galaxy and all the others believe the UGFS has their best interests at heart, but large pieces of it are corrupt, run by the Denards themselves. It's time we stop letting them control us. It's time we stop letting them do whatever they wish to all of us without any consequences."

Rio stood, his black eyes fixed on Yarza. "But what is the Denards' ultimate goal? Do we even know? Is it even worth us fighting when in the long run it will only lead to more suffering?"

Yarza leaned forward, his gaze boring into Rio's. "Does it matter what their ultimate goal is when they do things like create and spread the G-Pox? Or when they have facilities like Telvin where they torture and destroy innocent lives?"

Rio glanced at the other Guavivas, a silent

conversation happening between them. He turned back to Yarza. "I suppose it doesn't. Not really. We're merely afraid they'll out the Guaviva secrets."

Tiger-man stood, slamming a clawed fist into the table. "We're all afraid the Denards will out our secrets. I have no doubt they know more about each of our species from the experiments they were doing than we may even know ourselves. My kind aren't much into the sciences. We're simple people. We just want to be left alone."

Yarza's eyes darkened, his metal face remaining expressionless. "All the Gartians ever wanted was to create and sell our alloy in peace. We never challenged the Denards, never threatened them in any way that we know of. And still they set the G-Pox upon us, nearly wiping out our entire species. If any of you think your kind is safe because you don't think you're a threat, you'd be wrong."

"But what do they want?" The words slipped from my mouth. "We have suspicions, theories, but no one knows for sure. I still don't know what they were trying to accomplish on Telvin. If they simply wanted power such a place wouldn't have existed."

"They were studying us. All of us," Eron chimed in. "Maybe partly to find our weaknesses, but that wasn't the only reason. Why would they create Mazatimz assassins? Why would they need something like that? There are plenty of other ways to kill, most of them easier and more efficient."

"The whys don't matter at this time," Yarza said. "We may never know why the Denards seek to destroy so many, and merely control others. They've wiped out entire species. Obliterated planets. No, the whys don't matter. We just need to stop them."

Rio crossed his arms over his chest. "And all you're asking of us is to spread the word, to educate our own kind?"

Yarza nodded. "For now."

"Fine. Then for now, we will do as you ask. It's in the Guavivas' best interest to do so. But make no mistake, we will protect ourselves at all costs. If we must choose our own safety over others, we will."

Tiger-man's claws scraped along the table, his fangs glinting when he snarled, "Does that mean you'll expose what the rest of us are doing if it comes to it?"

"No, of course not. But we'll run if we have to. We don't wish to engage in any kind of war."

Yarza sat, leaning back in his chair. "It won't come to that. Not a full-out war."

His words seemed to appease everyone, silence falling over the room. A few minutes later, without another word, Yarza rose, confidently striding out the way he came in.

A Gartian I didn't know stood. "We will arrange for safe passage to the destination of your choice for all of those who require it. Please follow me."

"I guess the meeting is adjourned," I mumbled.

It didn't feel like much of anything had gotten accomplished. Yarza left the information out that Ash had proof of other transgressions the Denards had done. It wasn't merely going to be word of mouth in regards to spreading the news of their treachery. Maybe that fact would have made Rio and the others less nervous. It wasn't my secret to tell, and I had to wonder if Yarza had a reason for remaining tight-lipped for the moment. Perhaps it was because Ash was missing.

I rubbed my temples, grimacing. *I'm getting a damn headache.* Politics weren't my forte. I had to focus on finding Zula. Now that our guests were no longer our guests, we were free to track her down.

"We need to have stills of the escape pod from the surveillance feed run through the computer so we can find Zula before something bad happens to her."

Masha tugged on my sleeve. "Zar went to do it. I think you pissed him off though."

I couldn't keep myself from rolling my eyes. "I told him I didn't mean anything by what I said. Who would have thought a big, bad Gartian would be so sensitive?"

Masha scowled. "What does size have to do with emotions?"

I threw my hands up in the air. "Not you, too." Since when was everyone so sensitive? I was beginning to understand why Jane had stopped caring about such things.

As if my thoughts of her conjured Jane, she flamed into the room, her clothes hanging from her body in burned and tattered clumps. "Tamzea! I need you!"

Normally I would have questioned her, but her appearance left no room for anything but action. "Lead the way." I had a feeling I knew why she needed me, and it wasn't for her. I didn't say anything to Eron, I knew he'd go wherever I went.

We sped through a maze of hallways, bursting outside, sprinting past Gartians going about their daily business. A few stopped to stare with curiosity. I paid no heed to them or where we were going; I simply focused on Jane, letting her direct my pathway.

Jane paused outside a large glass building, not even out of breath. "Hurry! Please hurry!"

She sprinted into the entrance and down a long hallway, darting into one of the rooms on the right. I took a moment outside the door to catch my breath, and to steel myself for whatever I'd find inside.

Eron slid up beside me, taking my hand in his. "We'll handle it together. We're stronger, remember?"

Nodding, I stepped into the room.

Chapter 27

Ash's prone form was sprawled across the small bed, his chest bare and bloody. A gaping wound just south of his heart oozed black-tinged blood. His eyes were open, but rolled back in his head, his breathing ragged. His normally bronzed skin was sallow, his dark hair plastered to his head. One didn't have to have my kind of abilities to know he was at death's door.

"You have to heal him!" Jane shouted, very near hysterics. "I can't go— He can't— Don't let him die!"

My astonishment and despair were instantly replaced by calm. "Tell me what caused the wound." Striding forward, I assessed the state of his energies, zeroing in on the problem. He wasn't healing, obviously, but something was sucking away his power, something keeping his extraordinary phoenix healing abilities from mending his own body.

"I'm not sure. He was like this when I found him. Whoever did it left him for dead. But the only thing I know of that can kill a phoenix like this is a special kind of blade—"

"Yes, I remember."

"There's a piece of something in the wound. Deep inside," Eron said, his gaze focused on Ash.

Instinct kicked in. "We need to get whatever it is out. I can feel something sucking away his power, which is why he isn't healing. Maybe what's left in there is the problem."

Kneeling beside Ash, I felt his forehead. He was ice cold. Not a good sign for a phoenix. "Jane, go to The Pittsburgh and get my kit. We don't have much time. We have to open him up, it's his only chance."

"Don't you dare let him die." She flamed away, disappearing right before my eyes.

"Jane," Ash murmured, grimacing in pain.

I smoothed Ash's hair back from his face. "He's not coherent but he senses she's gone."

"Jane!" He arched up, screaming in agony.

"Here." Jane reappeared, shoving my silver medical kit at me.

Spreading it out before me, I grabbed a scalpel and tweezers. "Eron, you keep the healing energy flowing, and keep him calm, while I open him up. We don't have time to sedate him. Once I get whatever it is out of the wound, hopefully we'll be able to fix him."

Nibbling the inside of my lower lip, I cut into the wound. Ash screamed, collapsing, unconscious almost instantly. *Good.* My job would be easier without him writhing in pain while I dug around in his chest. I needed to save all of my energy for healing and not waste it on pain relief.

"I see it." Without time for finesse, I plunged the tweezers into the wound, trying to snag the end of something metallic. I would have missed it if I hadn't sensed the general placement of the foreign object already.

Jane dropped to her knees on the other side of Ash, taking his hand. "Hang in there, okay? I know you can hear me. Just hang in there. I won't lose you. I can't." Flames whipped along her arm, jumping to his, heating his body.

"Shit." I dropped the tweezers, the metal burning the tips of my fingers. "Jane, I can't work if you do that." The blisters instantly healed, an easy fix for a Mazatimz, and I bent over the tweezers on the ground, blowing on them.

Jane dropped Ash's hand, hanging her head. "I can't control it."

I grunted, scooping up the tweezers, which were still warm, but manageable. "Okay, I'm going for it. Do what you can, Eron."

Power surged through me, warm and comforting. It soothed my nerves, reassuring me. *I will save him.* Placing one hand on Ash's chest, I plunged the tweezers back into the wound. *Just missed the heart. I need to be careful.* Twisting down and then up, with a sucking sound, the object popped free.

"It's the end of a blade," Jane hissed.

I snagged Eron's hand, and closed my eyes, directing all of my power into Ash, imagining his body knitting back together. Golden light danced behind my lids, and joy filled me to the brim. I knew what to do now that the blade was out.

"Jane, burn him. Share your flame with him. He needs you."

My eyes snapped open as Eron tugged me back, fire bursting forth from Jane, covering Ash completely. The heat of it was like nothing I could ever imagine, and as I watched Ash's chest completely mend, I couldn't help but be in awe.

Ash abruptly sat up, pulling Jane to him, and covering her lips with his. It was then I noticed both of their clothes had burned away, and Ash was … very happy to see Jane.

"I think they're good." I giggled, my mood suddenly buoyant. *We did it. We saved Ash.* I squeezed Eron's hand, grinning at him.

A loud and long moan filled the air from Jane. Averting my eyes, I headed straight for the door. *Yep, they're better than good. Mission accomplished.*

Once in the hallway, with the door closed securely behind us, I let what just happened fully sink in. I had so many questions. Where had Ash been? Who knew what he was and knew to use the type of blade that could kill a phoenix, let alone have one? On the bright side, if someone was so intent on killing Ash, then he was ruffling some feathers, which meant we were on the right track.

"How long until The Pittsburgh leaves?" Eron asked, his voice husky.

Lust hummed along through our bond. My eyes widened when I met his gaze. "Why?"

"Well ..." He leaned into me, brushing his lips along my jawline. I shivered. "I'm thinking if we have the time, Ash and Jane have the right idea."

I scrunched my nose up, even as heat burned through my veins. "Eww ... it's kind of weird, you know?"

Eron's hot breath fanned out along my cheek, his teeth nipping at my ear. "Why? We've been focused on so many other things, their reunion just reminded me that we haven't had a proper one." His fingers slid down along my spine, and he cupped my ass. "I really want one."

It was true. Eron and I needed a reunion of the naked kind. We'd had sex, but it lacked the intimacy I'd come to expect from him. Especially when things were done. When we'd coupled on Telvin, afterwards he'd just walked away. Our connection had never truly been broken, but there'd been a distance, a disconnect, up until I helped him with his block. The difference was there when he touched me, his power zinging along my skin, warming me from head to toe.

"I want one, too," I rasped, running my hands over his silky hair.

Eron spun me around, hustling me into the room right across the hall from Jane and Ash's, slamming the door shut behind us. He shoved me down onto the bed, and I flopped onto my back, scrambling to make the fall appear somewhat graceful.

"I missed you so much. I can't even begin to explain. So damn much." He pulled his shirt off, exposing his lithe muscles, and rock-hard abs. "I wondered," he swallowed, his eyes darkening, "so many times, uncountable times, if you were off with someone else, living a life, and starting a family, all because you thought I was dead. It drove me insane."

Sitting up, I grabbed the sides of his face, staring into the depths of his eyes. "I've never considered, not even once, being with anyone besides you. My life has been about healing and keeping my crew safe. You have to know, you have to feel it, I could never let anyone but you touch me intimately."

"They tried to force me ..." He stood, shaking his head as if to dislodge his current thoughts. "I don't know why I'm bringing this up now of all times."

My heart twisted, torn between telling him to forget about it and demanding to know what he was suggesting. "No, I need to know. What did Telvin try to force you to do?"

"There were other female Mazatimzs there at different points, all of them dead now. But during the first few years, they tried to make me ... mate with some of the females."

I ground my teeth together. "And what happened?"

Breathe. Just breathe. He said tried, *not* did. *Give him a chance to explain before you have a meltdown.*

"Umm … well …" He turned away, the tips of his ears flushing.

"Spit it out already! What happened?"

He cupped his crotch, displaying his erection through his pants. "Let's put it this way. This only works for you."

I stared at him, my cheeks heating. "Oh."

"Yeah." He tugged his pants down, exposing just how well his cock worked for me. "They tried drugs …"

"And nothing worked," I breathed, in complete awe.

"No, nothing. I only want you. I've only ever wanted you."

I thought back to when we'd been forced to be naked together at Telvin, and how difficult it'd been for the both of us. We'd been in a constant state of arousal, even though we'd fought it, needing to resist so I wouldn't get pregnant.

"Mmm …" I stripped, needing to feel every inch of him pressed against me. "Come here."

Eron walked on his knees up the bed, his cock bobbing with each move he made. My mouth watered. *He's so beautiful. And he's all mine.*

Without any warning, he grabbed my inner thighs, forcing my legs apart, and fell on me with his mouth. "I forgot how good you taste." His gaze locked with mine just as he sucked on my clit. I cried out, arching off the bed. My focus narrowed down to the tiny bundle of nerves he concentrated his ministrations on, all sense of anything else falling away. He lapped and sucked, using his fingers and mouth to wring pleasure from me.

"Come for me, Tamzy," he rumbled, the vibrations driving me mad. "I need to feel you come for me like this." As if his command alone forced it on my body, my toes curled, and my heels dug into his back as I came almost painfully, stars dancing in front of my eyes.

"That's right, so beautiful," he purred.

Boneless, I sank into the bed, luxuriating. Before I had a chance to gather my thoughts, Eron pushed my arms over my head, capturing my wrists with one hand. He grinned, his lavender eyes lost in the black of his lust-blown pupils. I screamed when he plunged into me, grinding his hips in a slow circle.

"Eron, too sensitive, need a minute," I blathered, wiggling underneath him.

"Sorry, I can't wait."

"Unnng … bllaaampph …" Nonsensical things spilled from my mouth as I was swept away in pleasure again.

He pounded into me, giving me no reprieve, despite my request. Covered in a fine sheen of sweat, I tore at his back with my nails, screaming his name over and over. He caught my lower lip between his teeth, biting. Pain and pleasure blended, and I didn't care which one Eron delivered as long as he didn't stop touching me.

A faint tingling had begun in my forearm, hardly noticeable at first with everything else going on. But somewhere between my third and fourth orgasm, the sensation morphed into something akin to being branded by a red-hot poker. Glancing at the offending area, my eyes widened in amazement as I witnessed a mark forming there … a snake just like Eron's.

I turned my attention back to Eron himself, staring into his eyes. He was wide open to me in that moment, and in an instant, everything he'd experienced at Telvin flashed in my mind's eye. In theory, the horrors should have been unpleasant, but instead, it was a sharing of our souls, an understanding on the deepest level possible. For that reason, seeing the atrocities was a joyous thing, and I fell over the edge, reveling in yet another orgasm, knowing that Eron was truly mine again—each and every piece of him, the good and the bad.

"I love you … fuck … I love you." Eron dropped down on top of me, his face sliding into the crook of my neck as he pulsed his release into me.

We lay there, hearts thrumming erratically, and our sweat cooling, causing us to stick together. I ran my hands in small circles along his back, healing the raised welts I'd left there.

"I never thought I'd have you like this again. I never thought …" Eron clutched me to him while still inside of me.

Clinging to him, I squeezed my eyes shut, wanting to lose myself in Eron forever. Our Metza bond burned bright between us, stronger than it'd ever been before. When we'd barely been out of adolescence we hadn't suffered any hardships. Our bond had been strong, but after all, we'd been through at the hands of Telvin, how we'd almost lost each other … we were unbreakable now.

"I love you, too," I whispered, wanting to say the words even though I knew they weren't necessary. I was sure Eron could feel my love for him, burning brighter than it ever had before.

Chapter 28

"I didn't know such a thing was possible." Eron traced the snake tattoo on my arm. It was identical to his in every way. His had faded a bit as if he'd shared some of the coloring with mine.

I lifted my head from his bare chest, meeting his gaze. "I'm not sure what it means, but I know it makes me happy."

Eron shook his head in amazement, chuckling. "I don't understand any of this, but yeah, it makes me happy, too. Which is odd because I never wanted any of this for you. I never wanted you to know about the things I did on Telvin, at least not in detail. I—"

"We're in this thing together." I grinned, my mood jubilant. I decided it wasn't necessary to tell him that I'd already known bits and pieces from my nightmares.

"What thing?"

"Life, duh."

Eron rolled his eyes, dropping my arm to shove me onto my back. “That’s corny.” He grinned. “But I’ll take it.” Slanting his lips over mine, he kissed me tenderly. I moaned into his mouth, raising my pelvis in an open invitation.

Five sharp raps sounded from the door. “Hey!” Jane called. “We’ve been looking everywhere for you two! Put some clothes on and get your asses on The Pittsburgh. Dar has the information to track the pod Zula was in.”

“Be right there!”

Eron groaned, rolling off of me. “Back to reality, I guess.”

Jane was waiting for us outside the door when we emerged, dressed in an elaborate Steampunk outfit complete with a top hat. I stared in disbelief.

“Well, well, well, I didn’t know you had it in you.” She tilted her head, a smirk stretching her lips. “Or maybe I did.”

“How’d you know we were in here? And what’s up with your outfit? A bit overkill, don’t you think?”

She straightened her clothes, wiggling with pride. “New acquisition. Thought I’d dress for the occasion of bringing Zula back.” She turned, walking with extra pep.

Eron wrapped his arm around my waist, and I leaned into him, following Jane. “When did you have time to shop?” The middle part of her outfit, a corset I think she’d called it before, had tails with a gear pattern in gold detail along the edges. I glanced down at my simple black pants and top, wondering if I needed something fancier now that Eron was back in my life. I didn't have anyone to impress before, but now I did.

"There's always time to shop. I've told you, this is important for my business."

Eron looked at me with question and I shrugged. "You never said how you knew where we were?" Did she knock on every door in the building? I couldn't help but be curious at Jane's antics, they were amusing ... most of the time.

"Oh, well ..." Jane erupted into a fit of laughter.

"What?"

Choking back her glee, she turned, walking backwards while she stared at me with mirth dancing in her eyes. "Of course, we checked the room the Gartians gave you to stay in first. Then we checked all the common areas. After that, we asked if anyone had seen you. And then while we were formulating a plan on how exactly to track you down since you two seemed to have disappeared into thin air ..." She snorted, her mouth twisting as she attempted to contain a huge grin. "A report came in, from a Gartian who'd been patrolling, of loud ... noises coming from an unoccupied room in the medical building." She raised her eyebrows waiting for my reaction.

"Loud noises?"

"Yep, moaning, and screaming, and—"

"I get it!" My cheeks heated, and I turned my face into Eron's side, wanting to disappear. There wasn't the tiniest chance Jane would ever let me live this one down.

"I, of course, knew immediately who was in that room.

Especially when someone kept screaming out 'Eron! Eron! Oh, yes, Eron!' for starters." She winked at Eron. "I'm impressed you could get our meek little Tamzea to be so—"

"Shut up!" I hissed. "We should be talking about finding Zula."

"Oh, we're going to find her, and when we do we're going to have to explain to her that our little Tamzea is a freak between the sheets. I'm sure Zula will have tons of questions because you know how she loves to have data on everything. Heaven forbid facts regarding sexual behavior about Mazatimzs not be known by her and her huge brain. She'll probably take notes." Jane swiveled around, doubling over with laughter. "Oh, this is going to be good."

"What about you and Ash? You didn't even want to catch feelings for him. He seduced and mated you against your will. Eron and I have been bonded Metzas since childhood. It's only natural ..."

Jane howled with laughter, causing my retort to be lost in the raucous sound.

We hastened onto The Pittsburgh, Jane continuing to howl even as she made her way to the control room. I glared daggers at her back before heading to the medical wing with Eron. I was itching to do inventory after using up a lot of what we had on our guests.

"Get ready for takeoff. Thirty-minute warning," Jane announced over the intercom. "And Tamzea, make sure you're strapped down. Underneath Eron doesn't count."

"Oh!" I hurled the closest thing to me at the intercom, which turned out to be an empty translator package. "She's never going to stop. Never."

Eron chuckled, settling himself into a metal chair, and stretching his muscular legs out. He pulled the journal we'd stolen from Telvin out from under the chair, where he'd had it stashed.

I'd forgotten about the journal. Now my curiosity was officially piqued again. "What's so important about that thing?"

Eron ran his hand over the smooth red cover, his face grim. "This isn't the original. This thing, or a copy of it, is kept by Denards, kind of like the human *Bible*, but not quite. It's sort of an origins tale, I suppose. They don't let just anyone read it. Which is why it's important. It holds vital information about the Denards. Information that might help us fight them in the long run. Maybe it'll even clue us in to their motivations. I first found out about it from a fellow Telvin resident. I'm not sure how he got his information, but he's dead now so he won't be letting me know."

Plopping down into the chair next to him, I took the journal from him, inspecting it. The cover was red, with no markings or title. When I flipped it open, the scrawl inside appeared to be handwritten, but upon further inspection, it was clearly a copy, just like Eron said. I couldn't read the language though.

"I didn't know you could read the Denard language."

"I can't, not exactly, but I've figured out a way around

that little problem." I tilted my head in question. "I may not understand the words, but I've figured out how to sound out the syllables. If I say the words softly to myself, my translators do all the work."

I blinked a few times. "That's ingenious."

He grinned. "I know."

"Let me know if you find anything interesting." I reluctantly left his side, deciding to get started on the inventory I was itching to do. Eron mumbled to himself, the words too low for me to make out what he was saying.

Humming, I glanced back at Eron every so often, smiling every time I did. It was a different kind of satisfying to have him near me, the two of us doing our own thing, and yet the thread of our bond holding us together tightly.

About fifteen minutes passed, and I was completely focused on organizing the meds and supplies, when Eron jumped to his feet, letting loose a string of obscenities.

"What? What did you find?"

Eron ran a hand through his hair, his lavender locks spiking up at odd angles. "I'm not sure if I believe what I just read. But … I— It's something I would never have considered in a billion years."

Slamming the metal locker shut, I bounced up and down, eager for him to share. "What? Just spill it already!"

"The Denards are human."

I blinked rapidly, my brain not processing the words. I opened and shut my mouth a few times, but nothing came out.

"I told you it was hard to believe."

Hard to believe? Try near impossible. "What do you mean *human*?" As far as I knew, or the rest of the Universe knew, humans were a thing of the past. Spliced humans, who let's face it, were only half-human, were all that was left of the species that once inhabited Earth.

"I mean human. As in human." He paced back and forth between the chair he'd been sitting in, and where I hovered near the supply locker.

I grabbed his arm. "You need to explain."

He blew out a long breath, staring down at the journal in his hands. "I haven't gotten very far in this thing yet. I'm almost afraid of what I'll find if I keep reading."

"Okay, but what did you find so far? What makes you think the Denards are human?"

"The author of the journal talks about the discovery of aliens for his people. He goes on to say how up until that point humans had been at war with themselves constantly over things such as perceived race differences, religion … you name it. But when other life forms were discovered they were afraid."

"Right, which is how spliced humans came about. I already knew that."

"Mmm … well, apparently not all agreed with that plan. A militant group of humans, yeah, that's right, called the Denards, wanted to keep the bloodlines pure. They thought by splicing, humans would no longer, in fact, be humans." Eron flopped back down in the metal chair. "They're the ones who destroyed Earth. Or that's what I think. I haven't gotten that far in yet, but the author alluded to a plan to wipe out the abominations. It sounds to me as if the Denards developed a hatred for their fellow humans, the ones who opposed them, and for all things Earth. They considered themselves superior to the other humans. This journal," he rapped his knuckles against the hard shell, "is the original story of the Denards, told through the point of view of one of the founding members. Its tone is just as you might expect."

I pressed my palms into my eyes and rubbed. "The origin of a species who are really just humans? The last pureblood humans in existence." If my mind was a computer it'd be smoking. "How do we know any of it is true?"

"Why wouldn't it be?"

He had a point. Why would a species such as the Denards, who hated half-humans, and everything to do with Earth, want to have origins on Earth themselves? "No wonder that thing was under lock and key. Why would they even keep it? Why not erase all evidence of their human heritage?"

"I'm sure there's more to it than that. I need to keep reading."

"You're right. It can't be that simple. There has to be more information in that thing." Maybe we'd gotten lucky and we'd get all the answers about the Denards we'd been searching for. After all, it was easier to figure out someone's motivations if you knew where they came from, and where their heart was.

"I'm going to keep reading." Eron flipped open the journal to where his thumb had been holding his place.

I nibbled my bottom lip. "Do me a favor, okay?"

Eron didn't look up. "Hmmm?"

"Let's keep this whole human thing between us for now. At least until we have all the information. I'm not sure Jane would take it all that well, being that she is part human herself."

"No problem." He began reading again, his lips moving to form the words so they could be translated.

Jane's voice crackled over the intercom. "We really are taking off now. I was just prepping everyone before. Especially Tamzea, I figured thirty minutes was enough time to wrap up whatever was going on." She cackled demonstratively, the intercom then going silent. It popped back on a second later, and Jane said, "And we're going to be hopping right into a light slide once we're in space. So get ready. This is the real deal."

The floor vibrated, signaling lift-off before everything equalized out. "We better buckle in." Each of the chairs and beds were equipped with straps for takeoff, in case someone couldn't be moved, or for me, of course. Just as Eron and I managed to secure ourselves, my vision wavered for a moment, and I knew we'd gone into a light slide. I used to get spacesick every time The Pittsburgh dropped into a light slide, but I'd learned to soothe myself rather quickly. I still got a bit of vertigo, though.

"Mmm ... come here." Eron pulled me against his side,

his lips grazing my temple, immediately easing my dizziness.

I heaved a sigh of relief. Everything would be fine. Jane had Ash back, Masha and Dar were good, and I had Eron, *my* Eron back. I had complete confidence that Zula would be found soon, and—

KABOOM! The ship wobbled, the lights flickering before the backups blinked on.

Confused, I unbuckled myself, hitting the button on the intercom. "What's going on? What was that?"

"Hold on tight. We're under attack," Jane responded, her tone clipped.

Fear raced up my spine, and I hurried back to my seat, buckling myself in again. "Someone had to be waiting for us to catch us straight out of a light slide, which is the only time we can't use the cloaking device."

A series of small explosions boomed in the distance. I couldn't tell if we were being fired at, or if it was us retaliating.

"It'll be fine," Eron muttered, his tone belying his nerves.

Nausea rolled through my gut, blind fear causing me to panic. It was the not knowing what was happening that was terrifying. One ship could be attacking us, or a thousand. They could have the intent to capture or kill. And there was the matter of who was attacking. Sadly, there were too many options to make a truly educated guess.

"I can't lose you again," I muttered into Eron's shirt.

He threaded his fingers into my hair, tugging my head back so he could meet my gaze. "You won't. I promise."

"You can't make that promise. Not really." My heart quadrupled in time when The Pittsburgh shook, lights flickering again. I clutched at Eron, digging my fingers into his shoulders, holding on for dear life.

"Look at me, Tamzy. Just focus on me."

"I can't. I can't lose you. I want off this ship. I can't deal with this anymore."

"I said to look at me."

Despite my downward-spiraling emotions, his tone commanded me to obey, and I did. His lavender gaze held me captive, and before I knew what was happening, his lips had me ensnared as well.

Surrounded by his scent, immersed in his taste, and the feel of his hard muscles under my fingertips, I was swept away from worry, lost in rapture ... because I needed to be.

"You've got to be kidding me," Jane's voice yanked me from reverie.

Blushing, I turned to see her glaring at me. "The Pittsburgh was under attack and you two thought it was a good time to make out? And you always tell me you don't know how humans survived at all, let alone half-humans like myself. Right back at you, Mazatimzs."

I cleared my throat and unbuckled my belt, standing on wobbly legs. "Eron was trying to distract me. You know how I get in tense situations. I was a step away from a meltdown."

"Oh, ye have little faith in me, huh? Sure, we were under attack, but I had everything under control."

I swallowed, clutching for the chair and missing. Luckily, Eron grabbed my arm before I could fall. "It was that close? Who was after us this time?"

Jane crossed her arms over her chest. "I just said I had everything under control."

"Which is what you say when you don't have anything under control. You forget how well I know you."

"Pffft … I did have everything under control this time."

Ash appeared behind her, lifting a brow sardonically, his handsome face glowing with delight at the prospect of teasing her. "She didn't. But thanks to me now everything is under control." Jane swatted at him, and he laughed good-naturedly.

"Anyhow," Jane said, scowling at Ash, "a small, unmarked ship was waiting for us when we dropped out of our light slide. We volleyed fire for a few minutes, which I'm sure you're aware of, and then they stopped suddenly. We cloaked The Pittsburgh and made a run for it."

"Jane," Masha's voice came over the intercom. "We're being hailed by Nina."

"Nina?" Jane glanced at Ash. "I've been wondering where she disappeared to." She pressed the intercom to respond to Masha. "What does she want?"

"She says she has Ambassador Aralias captive, and she wants to put him in our prison."

"What? Ambassador Aralias is dead," I blurted.

Jane blinked rapidly, staring through me when she mumbled, "I knew it was too easy. It always is." She punched the intercom button again. "Tell her to bring him, and only him, via the airlock. I'll be happy to lock up Ambassador Aralias. Very happy indeed." A menacing smile spread across her face. "Coming?"

Curiosity overcame me. Supposedly the ambassador was dead. He was the Denard responsible for kidnapping and torturing Jane. He was also the reason Nina's face was covered in scars, which hadn't made it unbelievable when she claimed to have killed him, despite her status as his wife. "Of course I am. I wouldn't miss it."

"Good." Jane stalked from the medical wing on a mission, the rest of us trailing behind.

Things are never boring around here. Why did I think I'd get a moment of peace with Eron before something crazy happened again?

Chapter 29

Dar peered into the airlock, his hulking frame blocking everyone else's view. Jane and I alternated attempting to see around him, to no avail, and Ash and Eron stood behind us, talking in low tones about who knew what. They were probably starting a support group to deal with Jane and me. Masha, of course, was ensconced in the engine room, content to let Dar take care of things. Or probably, Dar, as a Gartian was eager to get his hands on Ambassador Aralias, a Denard he was permitted to insult and possibly harm.

"Dar!" I shoved at his side, annoyed that it didn't do any good. "Stop hogging the window."

"What she said, but as an order, from your captain!" Jane hissed.

Dar didn't heed either of us, standing his ground. "They've entered the airlock," he rumbled. "It's equalizing now."

I grunted with displeasure, wanting to watch for myself. "Please, Dar. Jane and I could both watch if you'd just move." I shoved at him again. "Jane's your captain, and I have crew seniority and ranking … just move!"

"I don't understand why we're letting him on this ship," Dar growled, his metal hand scraping down the wall. "Or her again for that matter. We could jettison them out into space right now and be done with them for good."

"We're not jettisoning Nina," Jane and I said in unison.

Nina was a Denard, sure, but she was a good one, and for all we knew, the only good one. She'd saved Jane's life once, and I had a feeling if I would have stopped to listen to her warning about the twins, they never would have managed to abduct me. Nina didn't deserve the hostility Dar consistently directed at her. Although there was the question of the ambassador still being alive when she'd supposedly killed him. Maybe she'd left him for dead and assumed his ultimate demise. Everyone knows how well doing that works out … essentially it seldom does.

"All right. That's it." Jane brandished her laser gun, shoving it into Dar's ribcage. "Get out of my way or I'll shoot. I won't kill you. I'll make sure I aim for a place Tamzea and Eron can heal you, but damnit, Dar, I'll do it. I'll so do it. I'm your captain and you're supposed to listen to me. If you choose not to then I'll damn well make you any way I can."

I sniggered when Dar reluctantly sidestepped, muttering about any creature with human blood being insane. Eron moved up beside me, wrapping an arm around my waist, pulling me back a few steps. "Hey! What do you think you're doing?"

"Keeping you safe." He kissed my temple before scooting us back a few more steps.

"There's no danger. I just want to see what's going on."

Ash rolled his eyes. "You've been around Jane for too long. I'm convinced her curiosity is going to get her into trouble I won't be able to get her out of one day." He disappeared in a puff of smoke, apparently the only one not interested in watching the arrival procession.

"I'm letting them in, be ready." Jane punched the code eagerly, the door sliding open a second later.

Nina strode forward, still in her space suit minus her helmet, leading the ambassador by a chain. Also in a helmetless space suit, his arms were bound in the chain that attached him to Nina. His face was bruised and bloody, his eyes darting around to all of us before settling on Jane.

"Ah, Captain Wexis, a pleasure to see you again."

"This time the pleasure will be all mine." Jane motioned to Nina. "Come on, let's get him in a cell and then we're all going to have a little chat."

Nodding, Nina led the ambassador away, who managed to keep his head high despite the fact he was in chains.

Dar stared after them, hatred glowing in his eyes. "I still say we jettison them into space."

Ignoring Dar, Jane set after Nina, and I tugged Eron along as I tried to keep up. I wanted to hear what Nina and the ambassador had to say for themselves. The Denards had been cast in a mysterious shroud from day one, and now that Eron had discovered their human origins, they seemed less threatening somehow. Humans were weak, breakable, and considered the bottom of the food chain. *And yet the Denards have terrorized this and every other galaxy since the formation of the UGFS.*

Eron and I hovered near the prison entrance, staying out of the way as Jane set up the grid around Ambassador Aralias' cell. The censors flashed on, the red crisscrossing lights glowing around the perimeter, making it next to impossible for the ambassador to escape. Not that a mere human possessed any special abilities.

"I will make you pay for this, Nina," Aralias snarled.

Nina notched her chin up, narrowing her eyes. "You've made me pay quite enough over the years." Her hand traced along one of the larger scars on her face. "And to think I ever thought I loved you."

"You're a traitor to the Denards, your own kind. Your father won't deny me your death when he hears of this."

Her eyes darkened, sparking with rage. "It's a good thing no one outside of this ship will ever hear anything from you again."

The ambassador laughed, the sound causing chills to race up my spine, and I gripped Eron's hand tighter. "It's him, isn't it? That hu-mutt you tainted yourself with before we were married? I know he was on this ship. I know you saw him." He stood, his face contorted into a mask of hatred. "I won't just kill you. I'll make you watch me torture and kill him first. I'll pick him apart piece by piece. And he'll die knowing it was all because of you."

Nina stared at the ambassador, her expression blank. Then she abruptly left the prison without another word.

Jane tapped the end of her laser gun against the outer bars. "Be talking to you soon, Ambassador Aralias. Tah-tah." She waved her fingers and smiled, leaving the prison, and snagging my arm on the way out. "Let's go," she hissed, "time for that crew meeting."

I glanced over my shoulder at the ambassador, studying him with curiosity. I'd read and heard stories of how pureblood humans had a cruel streak a mile long, but I never thought I'd meet one, having believed the pure lines to be extinct. And most species in the Universe thought their extinction was a good thing. Too bad we'd all been wrong, and they'd been hiding in plain sight, with an unknown agenda to boot.

I can't believe Jane is partly the same species as him.

ME, Eron, Dar, Masha, Nina, Jane, and Ash sat around the table in the eating lounge. It was Jane's preferred place for crew meetings. It felt weird without Zula there, though. I was even beginning to miss her lectures about … well, everything. The female knew how to talk, that was for sure.

"All right. Now that we're all here, it's time for Nina to explain where she was and what the hell happened."

"Why isn't Ambassador Aralias dead?" Masha blurted.

Dar narrowed his eyes. "The destruction of his ship was confirmed, and supposedly so was his death, which was why Jane believed you when you said you killed him."

I noted how he said 'Jane believed'. Of course, we all knew Dar didn't trust a damn word or thing Nina said or did. He wasn't the only Gartian, but Jane had insisted on taking her onto The Pittsburgh so there wasn't much to be done without definitive proof of her lying about anything.

"Just tell us what happened." I curled my hand into a fist, attempting to keep my bias under control. Humans were liars by nature. Plenty of species were capable of lying, but from most old accounts, none took pleasure in political backstabbing and machination like humans had since the conception of their race. Jane was a spliced human, and although most of the Universe didn't hold any respect for them either, I at least felt like their altered genetics gave them more of a chance to fight against the human part of their twisted DNA.

"I lied to you. I lied to all of you." She met each of our gazes in turn, before continuing. "I was sent to spy on you. The Gartians were right to mistrust me from the beginning. I—"

Dar slammed his fist into the table, lurching out of his chair. "Throw her into the cell next to her husband! I warned you! I warned all of you!"

"That's enough!" Jane was on her feet in an instant, her hand twitching over her laser gun. "We will hear what she has to say before we come to a decision as a crew."

Masha jumped up onto the table so she could whisper in Dar's ear, running her tiny hands over his back and shoulders soothingly. He finally dropped back into his seat, crossing his arms over his chest. Masha settled into his lap, wiggling to get underneath his arms. It was a smart move to keep him under control. Dar would never do anything to hurt Masha, and he'd have to fling her off of him to have another outburst.

"We good now? Yeah?" Jane glanced at each of us, her gaze lingering on Ash, something silent passing between them.

Ash cleared his throat, staring at Dar when he spoke. "I, for one, want to hear what Nina has to say for herself. It took balls to admit to us here like this that she lied."

Jane sat back down, her back rigid. "Go ahead, Nina. I hope this is good."

Nina shifted in her seat, the force of our gazes causing her to stare at the table. "Like I said, I was sent here to spy on you. But—" She lifted her gaze to Jane's. "Maddox."

Understanding washed over me. Nina had fallen for Maddox, the spliced human from New Earth who was part of their military, before she'd been married to Ambassador Aralias. After she'd weaseled her way onto The Pittsburgh, he'd shown up to bring Jane back to New Earth. Seeing her first love, possibly the love of her life, had changed everything. *Lucky for us.*

I wasn't sure if anyone else besides me understood

what it was like to see someone who you loved after such a long time. It reminded you of the person you were and the person you'd become. It brought up memories of desires pushed aside because life got in the way, and sometimes you realized what you would be willing to do to go back. I could never go back in time with Eron, to have things the way they were, and neither could Nina with Maddox, but—

I cleared my throat, standing tentatively. "I get what you're saying, Nina." I flicked my gaze to Eron, who gave me an encouraging nod. "Maddox, the man you love, changed everything when you saw him again."

Nina's fingertips ran along the pattern of scars on her right cheek. "I couldn't be my husband's puppet anymore. I wanted to be the girl Maddox fell in love with all those years ago. I wanted …" She swallowed back tears, her head drooping forward.

Jane snorted. "Good thing I didn't kill Maddox when I shot him back when we were teenagers."

"Jane," I chastised. Maddox had grown up with Jane, and they had quite a sordid history.

She threw her arms up in the air. "What? I'm just saying, if I would have accidentally killed him then we'd probably all be in deep shit right about now."

"So everything you did was for Maddox?" I asked Nina, hoping to prod her subtly to continue.

"Yes, in a way. I realized that it was time to take my revenge. I'd wanted it for so long … but I was afraid. Terrified actually." She picked at her nails, not wanting to meet anyone's eyes. "The ambassador abused me into complacency. And I was humiliated when I saw Maddox. I may never see him again, but if I do, I'll be able to look him straight in the eyes from now on."

"So you lied to us, got on The Pittsburgh, and were in the perfect position to continue being your husband's lackey, but boom, enter Maddox." Jane waved her hand for Nina to continue. "Then what?"

"Then I bided my time until I could do the most damage t-to *him*." Nina trembled with rage. "When the twins showed up I tried to warn Tamzea, but she wouldn't listen—"

"That's true," I interjected. "She did try to warn me, but I refused to hear what she had to say, and the next thing I knew I was waking up on Telvin."

"Right," Nina said. "So I let him know that Tamzea was at Telvin, hoping to lure him with the promise of finally catching Jane and Ash. When he showed up there I led him away from Telvin so I could spring my trap." She spread her arms wide. "And here we are."

"Why didn't you just kill him instead of bringing him here?" Eron asked, his eyes narrowed in blatant skepticism. "I know I'd kill someone like him the first chance I got, especially after the years of abuse." His gaze flitted over her scars demonstratively, his eyebrow quirking.

Nina looked to Jane instead of Eron when she responded. "Because he knows where Zula is."

"We have what we need to track Zula," Dar snapped. "I

say let's end the ambassador's miserable life and then light slide out of here."

Masha shushed him, and Jane waved him off with annoyance. "I assumed after what you said in the prison that nobody knows you have Ambassador Aralias and there's no way to track him?"

"As far as everyone is concerned, he died on his ship … again. We're the only ones who now know that he's alive." Nina smiled, her eyes darkening with promised violence.

Jane grinned at me. "You ready to play good cop, bad cop?"

Huh? "I'm not sure I know what you mean."

"It's a tradition for interrogation from Earth. I'll rough up the ambassador, and you can heal him so I can do it all over again."

Ash chuckled. "That's not how good cop, bad cop works, Janey."

"It is today, my whittle Ashby." Ash rolled his eyes at the nickname meant to annoy him.

"Okay, you know I'll do whatever I can to help Zula," I chimed in.

Eron grabbed my hand. "Not without me."

I leaned into him and murmured, "Of course not."

"Then let's get this party started!" Jane left in a blur of flame and smoke, laughter echoing in her wake.

As we made our way to the prison, I couldn't help but wonder if it was irony or not that Jane wanted to use an Earth method of interrogation on someone who was one-hundred-percent human, but she didn't know it. *Hmm …*

Chapter 30

"I'm going to ask you one more time—where's Zula?" Jane punctuated her question by pressing a burning hand against Ambassador Aralias' bare chest.

He screamed, writhing in agony, his eyes rolling back into his head as he slumped forward, unconscious.

Jane kicked his bare foot, sneering. "Heal him up nice and good again. And then we'll start all over. I'll be back in ten."

When she left, I exhaled in relief, rushing to the ambassador's side. Eron grabbed my shoulder before I could make contact. "Tamzy, you need to tell Jane how this is affecting you, or at the very least let me do it for you."

"No," I snapped. "I'm doing this for Zula. And we've had this conversation, you can't protect me from everything."

Eron wrapped his arms around my trembling body. "We're not meant to endure such things."

"Maybe not." I shoved him away from me, scowling. "But who is? Is any species meant to endure unpleasant things? Mazatimzs are coddled and sheltered, and on the whole unable to protect themselves ... just like when we were abducted from our home. Maybe if we'd been taught self-defense," my nostrils flared, "I don't know, but we could have had a chance."

"What are you saying?"

I dropped my gaze to the faint outline of the snake on my forearm, tracing it with my index finger. "I'm saying I will never enjoy torture or another soul's pain, but I'll do what I need to do to survive, and to keep everyone I love safe. I'll do what needs to be done."

"We're not like other Mazatimzs anymore."

"No. We're not. We're better." I closed the scant distance between us, tugging his lips down to mine.

Eron groaned into my mouth, attempting to deepen the kiss, but I pulled away. "Tamzy, I—"

"Now, shush and get out of my way. I have a human to heal, and a location to help discover."

"I love you."

"Of course you do, silly."

With more ease than ever before I healed Ambassador Aralias, stepping away just as his eyes fluttered open. Where burned and ruined flesh had been seconds ago, smooth, healthy skin was now visible. He stared down at his chest for a few moments in confusion and awe. "The

Mazatimz gift is amazing. Now you can see why we wanted to duplicate it."

"No, I can't see why you would need to duplicate it when we offer our services freely to those in need. We're not a power-hungry people."

"Ah," the ambassador lifted his head, dark locks falling into his brown eyes, "but we want it for ourselves."

"What are you talking about? Aren't your kind opposed to spliced humans?" Eron asked, astonishment making his lips loose.

Surprise intermingled with rage washed over the ambassador's exhausted visage. "We don't want to splice our genes, we want to steal the power."

What? No one could steal power from another species and use it in that way. My eyes widened, the blade that stole a phoenix's essence flitting across my mind. The magic in the blade stole the phoenix gift, and until that moment I'd assumed that was it. What if the blade was an attempt to steal the phoenix power for the Denards' personal use? What if they coveted abilities like New Earth humans, but they wanted them without having to tamper with their DNA?

I covered my mouth with my hand, backing away slowly. What if that's what Telvin was there for? What if the ambassador had just revealed the Denards' motivations without realizing it in his delirious state?

Jane's boots clumped up behind me. "Good, he's healed just in time for me to start all over again. But I'm thinking this will be the last time. If you two want to go now …"

"Going." I grabbed Eron's hand, yanking him after me.

"HOW MUCH MORE DO YOU have to read?" I nibbled my thumbnail while staring at Eron's profile. He was on my bed hunched over the Denard journal, his lips moving as he sounded out the words softly to himself.

He clenched his teeth. "I've gotten through one page since the last time you asked. If you keep pestering me it's going to take forever."

"I just want to have all the information before we tell Jane. And optimally I'll be able to talk things over with Zula before that. But it's not like we have a lot of time. Who knows when the next catastrophe will strike?"

Sighing, Eron set the journal on the table near my bed. "Come here."

"Why did you stop? Read! Read! Read, read, read!"

"I'll be able to read much faster when I'm relaxed. I can't concentrate with you breathing down my neck like you are." He grinned, flipping me onto my back. "And I have a solution that'll work for both of us."

I scowled even though my heart sped up, warmth blooming in my middle. "There's no time for that. You need to read the journal."

"Mmm hmm … I will. After I shut you up so I can concentrate."

"So now I talk too much?"

Eron dropped his body weight down on mine, ensnaring my lips with his.

"Buckle up, everyone, we're about to drop into a light slide." Jane's voice crackled over the intercom. "I have coordinates for Zula. Let's go get our girl."

My body relaxed just a little bit more knowing we were finally going after Zula. *We're going to be a family again.*

I threaded my hands into Eron's hair, and wrapped my legs around his hips, rocking against him. I sniggered against his skin, remembering how Jane had said being underneath Eron was not an acceptable way to strap in. I was about to test that theory.

Eron growled under his breath, the sound eliciting a shiver of pleasure from me. "Tamzy, baby, the mood I'm in right now … fuck, it's hard for me to be tender with you. I want to be, so damned much, but every time I have you like this …" He dipped his head, nipping at my neck.

Squirming against him, I dragged my nails down his back. "You've been tender—"

His sharp laugh cut me off, his lips moving against my overheated skin. "Ripping your pants down and fucking you in the control room from behind, yanking you into a spare room so I could ravage you first with my mouth and then—"

"Eron, please," I moaned. "Tender smender, I just want you any way I can have you."

His eyes darkened, glinting with lust. Without another word, he flipped me onto my stomach and slid my pants down. My fingers entangled in the sheets, and I groaned when his hands moved down my spine, settling on my hips as he lifted my ass into the air. His touch was rough, and demanding, but no matter what he said, tenderness was there underneath, burning brightly through our connection. He loved me, and I loved him, and no matter what had changed between us, that never would.

He plunged into me, and my mouth opened in a silent scream. His fingers bit into my flesh as he pounded in and out, in and out, his pace never wavering as he commanded my body to bend to his. My muscles suddenly spasmed as I hurtled into an orgasm, and I panted out Eron's name, his release following mine.

He pulled out and flipped me over, a smirk tipping one side of his mouth up. "That was just the appetizer. I plan on keeping you under me until this ship reaches wherever we're going." He trailed his index finger between my breasts and pressed his cock against my entrance again. "You have a problem with that?"

I shook my head, incapable of speaking with him looming above me like he was.

He grinned. "That's what I thought."

Epilogue

Sometimes the strongest creatures are the ones who love beyond all faults and fight battles no one else can see.

I'd opened up the block between Eron and his healing abilities, but he wasn't magically cured of the trauma he'd suffered. He hid it well, but every once in a while, it crept to the forefront of his psyche, and it was up to me to help him. I never minded. I loved him beyond all reason, without limitations. Besides, he wasn't the only one with issues. Maybe my trauma wasn't as severe, but I'd suffered, too, and there were times when it was his turn to hold me together. Just like always, together we could face anything. Which was a good thing because our adventures were just beginning.

Ambassador Aralias was truly dead this time. Jane burned his body until it was nothing but ashes, which she jettisoned into space. Dar had enjoyed that particular detail. But the ambassador would be missed, and his disappearance, along with Nina's, since she was no longer playing double agent, would probably open up questions we didn't want the Denards looking for answers to.

Once we safely had Zula secured on The Pittsburgh, our mission was clear: take down the Denards, and free the people of the Universe from the tyranny of the UGFS —the tyranny most of them had no clue they were being subjected to. They'd been lulled into false security, just like I'd been before Telvin had shown me another side of things. Somehow our little band of misfits would figure out a way to do it, I had confidence in us. Well, at least with the Gartians standing behind the cause as well.

Jane had finally stopped dragging her feet when it came to fully joining the cause, and all it had taken was for Telvin to mess with her crew. She realized she couldn't hide from the Denards forever, their reach seemingly extending into every darkened corner of the Universe. Her days of being just a bounty hunter were long gone.

Of course, there was still so much we didn't know. We were bound to run into plenty of trouble along the way. And there was the whole thing about the Denards being pureblood humans. When would be the right time to drop that bomb? If there was such a thing.

"Tamzea!" Jane yelled, pulling me from my inner musings. I hovered near the airlock, waiting for Jane to put on her helmet.

"Be ready, both you and Eron, in case Zula's injured."

"Of course."

Jane dropped her helmet down, snapping it into place. "I'll be back with our little Smurfette in a jiffy." She floated out of the ship, Ash zipping by her in flame form. She shook her fist at him, annoyed that he wouldn't take her with him because he wanted her to be more confident in her own flame form out in space.

Laughing, I turned away. "Those two are ridiculous."

"Mmm ..." My male of few words kissed me, causing my brain to temporarily short-circuit, and I lost myself in the only place I felt truly content: Eron's arms.

Acknowledgments

As an overthinker, acknowledgments are quite an arduous task for me. I wonder if I'm being lackluster or too intense with the thanks. Or did I forget someone? Possibly I gave too much credit to someone and therefore slighted someone else who actually did a ton. A part of me doesn't want to include these in my books at all because the people I appreciate should know it already … or do they??? No matter how I look at it these damn acknowledgments make me friggin' sweat.

But here they are anyways since if I don't include them then people will probably think I'm ungrateful and weird. I mean, I am weird, but I don't want people to think that. I am grateful though, so I'll just go-ahead and make this uncomfortable for everyone. Heh.

Okay, here I go. Right now. Actual acknowledgments to follow. Hopefully, they represent an appropriate level of gratitude to all the people in my life that deserve it.

(And yep … I have totally copy & pasted what comes next from my *Replayed* book acknowledgments, which I originally took from *Virtual Reality Bites* acknowledgments. I thought maybe after *Replayed* that I'd come up with something better. Or at least something new. Obviously not. So this is now copy & paste edition #4. Or 5? 6? Who even knows anymore. Therefore, I'm thinking you should probably get used to it.)

My amazing Hubby! Words can't begin to explain how supportive and truly amazing he is. Hmmm … I think I already used the word amazing. But unlike in books, when honestly applied to someone, the word amazing means something, well, amazing. And my hubby is all of the things that word implies. Romance heroes are nothing compared to him.

Lindsay Tiry … what would I do without you? I hope I never have to find out. From cover design to interior graphics to logos, you do it all. Your talent is awe-inspiring, and I hope one day everyone else will be able to appreciate how you shine.

Melissa Ringsted … my illustrious editor. Without you, this book probably would have gone straight into the trash. Thank you for giving me the confidence to publish when I convinced myself that I was the worst writer in the history of writers, and for fixing all the words.

Ren, Kristin, Shona, Ruty … my O.G. chicas … I wouldn't be here without you. I'm beyond lucky to know all of you.

And last, but certainly not least, thank you to everyone who has taken the time to read this book. Hopefully, you enjoyed it, but even if you didn't, I still appreciate the fact that with so many options out there today, you even gave my book a fleeting chance.

About the Author

Ava WIXX

Passion. Love. Chaos.

Ava Wixx escaped into books at a young age and decided to stay there. It was only a matter of time before she was driven to create her own fantasy worlds from fear of running out of places to explore.

Reader, writer, dreamer ... Ava only toils in reality when absolutely necessary. She lives in North Carolina with her husband, and spoiled mini-poodle.